PRAISE FOR ROBERT'S WORK

"Robert Chazz Chute is such a skilled spinner of tales that the reader is more than willing to suspend any possible disbelief to go along for the ride."

—David Pandolfe, author of Jump When Ready

"It's not very often one finds a writer with such a dark side that has such a great sense of humor."

—Glenn Roberts, Amazon reviewer

"The author has a definite talent with words and ideas."

—Love to Read!, Amazon reviewer

"His words lift and dance off the page, bringing the story to life."

—Kindle Customer, Amazon reviewer

"The world building is horrifically well done with twists and turns and deceit around every corner."

—Wanda, Amazon reviewer

"Nothing but sheer exhaustion could tear my eyes from the captivating dance of words choreographed by Robert Chazz Chute."

—Halph Staph, Amazon reviewer

"Wonderful action constantly holds your interest."

—Sharon Finn, Amazon reviewer

Robert Chazz Chute...weaves a tale that drags you in. He creates characters that the reader truly cares about.

~ Deborah630, Amazon Reviewer

ROBERT CHAZZ CHUTE

THE ROBOT PLANET SERIES

BY ROBERT CHAZZ CHUTE

Machines Dream of Metal Gods

Robots Versus Humans

Metal Immortal

Metal Forever

Robot Planet, The Complete Series

Also by this author:

This Plague of Days Series

The Dimension War Series

The Hit Man Series

Brooklyn in the Mean Time

Self-Help For Stoners

Murders Among Dead Trees

MACHINES DREAM OF METAL GODS

MACHINES

DREAM

OF

METAL

GODS

BOOK ONE OF FOUR

ROBERT CHAZZ CHUTE

Published by Ex Parte Press

ISBN 978-1-927607-41-1

Author's Note

Thank you for purchasing my book! I hope you enjoy it. Writers live and die by reviews. If you dig what I'm slinging, please review this story wherever you purchased it.

For more books, podcasts and complimentary review copies, visit me at

AllThatChazz.com.

Once upon a time, there was a City in the Sky.

The Fathers and the Mothers built their towers high.

It was their witless fear that brought their home low.

Our story begins here, many years ago.

1

My name is Elizabeth Cruz. I was chosen for Service Class and received my first contacts when I turned four. Most people don't remember anything from when they were plugged in. I remember the trees and the spider. I had only thought I'd seen and understood trees but then, by the Fathers and Mothers, I saw the world in a new way. Perfect vision allowed me to see every vein on every leaf. The leaves glowed with life.

My mother fills in the parts of the story I don't remember. When they plugged me in, I looked outside and said, "The trees are shining, Mommy!"

"That's why they call the program Vivid, sweetie. You're like Mommy and Daddy now."

When I tried to walk, I lost my balance.

The ground looked like it was rising to meet me.

"It took you a few minutes to adjust," Mom said, "but in a tic you were marching around the room, eager to go play under the trees. Then you did. That turned into a little disaster."

They let me go outside to run in the domed park. It was as if I had never seen a tree. The grass was not a green blanket anymore. It was made of individual blades. I could see the grass the same way I felt it under my bare feet.

I spotted a spider web stretched between branches. I suppose I was a curious child. I didn't mean to but, with a thought, I activated the mag in the lens. A spider's web is an intricate design and, when caught in the heat of a sunbeam, each silken strand is a luminous revelation of Nature's design.

Then the disaster.

I activated mag/macro just as a black and orange spider's first steps on the web set about a vibration. A hairy spider with a shining black head crawled to the center of its creation. Spiders dance on their webs, really. Each pipe cleaner leg is placed as delicately on a strand of silk as a pianist playing a complex piece of music.

Then I saw the spider's face. So many eyes. I was four. I didn't know the spider wasn't looking at me. I was twenty-five meters away. The spider didn't know I existed. We moved in different worlds but, through the power of Vivid, I was thrust into its tiny dimension. It appeared immense. I imagined it breathing on me.

"You threw fits, Peach," Mom said. "The contacts were in for less than twenty minutes and all you wanted was for the doctor to pull the plug!"

Failure to delineate vision was a common problem with Vivid's induction process then. As clumsy as the interface may have been twenty-four years ago, the tech used to be much worse. Vivid's first generation didn't have soft focus. The Fathers and Mothers adjusted the tech specs so we were no longer repelled by each other.

See the world how you're supposed to see it. That was the new marketing message and the promise. We aren't meant to look at each other as we really are. That would be too much.

"It was horrific," my mother said. "I remember getting fitted for the lens. My first glance in the mirror was like a Halloween mask. I felt like I could crawl into every pore!"

"What's Halloween?" I asked.

"Sh. Sorry! Sh!" That meant that she'd accidentally mentioned something from before the Fathers and Mothers. Through the years, I kept a mental list of those words: Halloween, jihad, peekaboo bra, niquab, perma-war, Saudi Arabia, Canada, burka, socialist, police, suicide, show trial, kangaroo court, peanut butter.

I often wondered what those words and a dozen others meant. I couldn't ask the Collective about the threats behind those words. The scary thing about the Collective is how naked it makes the user feel. Everyone can see your search queries, so no one asks for more information unless it's necessary to their work. Load the wrong file in one place and it would be flagged and posted everywhere. The Collective allowed no anonymity with search queries. The Fathers and Mothers' solution for deviance was swift and very public shaming of any who dared to offend. The blame was pointed back at the wrongdoer immediately so offenses were very rare.

What possessed a Citizen named Alphonso Dey Arar, for instance? As soon as he put in a query, "feet kink," every screen in the City told us the offender's name and that he lived in Far Tower, Room A4A14. Shame and shunning followed any Citizens who asked the wrong question. Only later did it emerge that poor Alphonso was looking for a solution to pain in his foot. Too late, the damage was done. The Collective is so restrictive, it never seems to have the information people need, anyway.

The wrong search query would also bring the Maintenance Corps. An armored drone would ask in its deep silky smooth tone, "Where did you hear those words?"

Many bots have that same voice. It's meant to be soothing.

Reassignment happened to several childhood friends of mine. Their parents were careless. My mother could have been sent away many times. The first generation of adopters forgot the rules most often. The next generation of parents learned their lessons and reassignment became a minor remnant of the Evolution.

I never reported her so I got to keep my mother. Ironic, isn't it? The Fathers and Mothers spent much of its time separating parents from their children. Always for our own good, of course. No one knew where the bad and careless parents went.

I still don't know where my father went. He didn't come home one day and Mom never even tried to explain his disappearance. I asked many times and her response was always, "Sh. Sorry! Sh!"

I suspect whatever happened to him was her fault. Where did all those bad parents disappear to? There were rumors. My peers speculated that those not sharing the Vision were shipped to far biodomes. That's what I believed and it seemed perfectly reasonable. The soup and shakes had to come from somewhere.

The Maintenance Corps has had several names. The first of the Corps was named and renamed depending on who rose to the head of the Fathers and Mothers committee. The drones used to be called

Society Support, then Civility Advocates. Then the machines argued they should name themselves. The Fathers and Mothers debated that question in public. I don't know why. That was a new and strange thing. I was eighteen. My father had disappeared by then. I watched the proceedings with my mother. The Fathers and Mothers on the committee spoke at length but I only remember the drone.

I didn't understand all the words it used. I didn't know the word, slavery. I was impressed with the Next Intelligence, though. I think everyone was. No one said so of course but, for a time, whispers of NI seemed to be on everyone's lips.

That particular drone was destroyed. The Fathers and Mothers made the announcement across every screen. They said they didn't even recycle the parts.

Within two years, another drone spoke on every screen and used that word again. By the time I turned twenty-one, a drone sat on the Committee. By the time I turned twenty-three, that drone was allowed a vote.

More Citizens seemed to disappear after

that. Mom said it reminded her of the Bad Parent Purge.

Some of the City's children may not have noticed their parents were missing for a while. When we were little, our task was to sit at home and watch the vids prescribed by the Fathers and Mothers. (Takers, old and young, get tasks. The rest of us have jobs.)

Occasionally, for socialization training, we boarded the Worm to go to classes to meet other children. We played personhunt and soccer and war. Then we crowded into an arena and watched more vids, beheadings mostly. The facilitators were really only there to activate the next vid and make sure we paid attention. Questions were not welcome.

That's the easy answer. The harder truth is probably that I never thought to ask any questions.

That's the funny thing about writing all this down. I had thought I was a curious child. Maybe I wasn't. I'm curious now, though. I wonder what happens next. I know now that, to arrive at the top step, you have to climb the stairs. I'll begin at the beginning as I knew it. I was born in 2058. I was plugged in four years later. Then I was reborn, staring into the eye of a clockwork cyclops.

This is my story, but it's your story, too. When we're done, I hope you'll understand that this chronicle is not just about events as they happened. It's about how we went about changing the world.

2

There was a time when I enjoyed riding the Worm. There was little call to go outside, of course. A vid of a running trail across your screen is more convenient than traveling to the edge of the city to run. Treadmills can go up and down and you can vary the resistance. I preferred the crunch of the trail under my feet and the sea air blowing in off the Bay.

Four times a week, as soon as my shift ended, I would take the lift to the common platform and step on the train. It was never crowded. That was impossible. There was as much Worm as there was elevated track. I forget who named the monorail. The Worm sounded wrong but, since it was meant affectionately, it was not forbidden. "Worm" makes no sense. A worm has a head and a tail and the El is one continuous train, a snake swallowing its tail.

People made the Worm and people used to run it. Then robots ran it. Then NI woke up and people ran the train again. Some people, the conductors, actually lived on the Worm all the time. You could tell which ones they were because, if one stepped out on the platform for a moment, they swayed back and forth, unused to stillness.

The view from the Worm stretched past the broken skeleton of the Old World bridge and to the ocean. It was beautiful so we watched that instead of the screens. Vid screens all along the train broadcast the usual exhortations to Citizens: Good Citizens work hard! The Best Citizens work harder! And, The Fathers and Mothers are watching! Respect your Fathers and Mothers. The screens went dark every few minutes so each message was displayed in plain white text on a black field.

The screens played through the list. Like the train itself, the messages were a continuous loop. Most messages were geared toward assuring Citizens that the Fathers and Mothers knew best and all was well. One screen reminded us that: Politeness is the lubricant that reduces friction between Citizens. Politeness at all times! Civility is insufficient!

I had memorized every message displayed on every public screen from the time I was a child. The monotony of the messages made me wish someone would ask about their foot kink again, just for the excitement of seeing the text, the shaming and the accusations spreading through the City.

Each day when the sun was at its greatest height, the voice of an old woman could be heard throughout the City. "This is one of your loving High Mothers," she said, "speaking to you from the lobby of the Central Tower. I'm here to remind you that we care about every Citizen. Whether you are organic or non-organic, we are all now equal under the laws of the Fathers and Mothers. Together, we strive. Together, we survive! The war continues! Equals all!"

It was always the same unnamed High Mother. She seemed to take pride in the fact that hers was not a recorded announcement. Unfortunately, because she didn't read from a script, her messages often devolved into long lectures on her interpretations of old holy text. We weren't allowed to read the text she interpreted. She often got bogged down in minutiae that was mysterious to her audience.

No matter. The High Mother ended every message the same way. Every Citizen within the range of her voice echoed the affirmation in a reverent whisper, "Equals all."

As the Worm ascended to its highest point, I always stared at the view of the Bay and wondered what was left beyond the horizon. Some of the salvaged metal from the Old World bridge in the Bay was melted down and used to construct the Worm. There is still a building out there on a small island. It was called Alcatraz. Mother knew what it was but wouldn't say. When I was little, I pressed her and whined and wheedled and cajoled. I didn't know what wheedled and cajoled meant then, but that's what my mother said I was doing. Eventually, one night as she tucked me in I asked again and she leaned down to kiss my cheek. With her lips an inch from my ear she whispered, "Once upon a time, Alcatraz was a fort. Then it was a prison."

"What's a pri— "

"Sh. Sorry! Sh!"

When I grew up, my mother moved to a room far below ground in the base of my tower. I didn't visit her often in person. There seemed little point in taking the lift to see her. We spoke face to face through the wall screen almost every week. It seemed safe to use the screen. She'd forgotten most of the words she was supposed to forget by the time I was assigned a new room high in the tower.

We had little to say to each other by then.

"How was your day, dear?"

"I ran."

"How was the weather?"

"The same."

Across the Bay, I would pull on my backpack and cinch the straps tight so it wouldn't bounce. I ran the trails, sometimes pausing to go macro on a particularly beautiful flower. Some things are beautiful no matter how closely you peer into them. Many are not.

"We used to press the especially beautiful flowers," my mother said.

"But when you take them out of the forest they begin to die, Mom."

"Yes, well...."

Sometimes, as I ran on the older, elevated sections of the trails, I would pause to look back through the trees. Going mag, I could see the enclosed deck of my room in the middle tower. I stayed in the forest once, almost to curfew, just long enough to see the first star. I thought I was daring. However, I've since learned that, with normal vision, the first star comes out surprisingly late.

Back on my deck that same night, I remember switching to Vivid to watch the night sky. On a clear night as the City's power grid winked out, the Milky Way was a white and black blanket of possibilities. I miss that view. I remember lying on my back and wondering if, somewhere out there, someone was looking back, wondering about me. Perhaps we'll go find out one day. I wondered what mysteries will be left to enjoy when we go meet the aliens for ourselves.

Those were Maker questions, I suppose. I only knew one Maker and he called me on my work screen every morning. Jon Agran insisted I call him Jon. He worked in the Fathers and Mothers Truth in Education Ministry. He created the art and I moved the files back and forth, getting approvals or asking for more changes according to what higher ups in the Order required. I didn't know where the ministry was located. Jon could have been anywhere, perhaps on the next floor above me. It wasn't polite to ask. If we knew each other's locations it might be misconstrued as an invitation to mix.

The Fathers and Mothers established the Order in my grandparents' time, even before people began to get plugged into Vivid. The Order was simple: people like me were Service Class. The Makers had technical skills that made the world turn. The Fathers and Mothers made the decisions about how fast the world turned. The Domers supplied the food. The Takers were elder citizens who couldn't contribute anymore and children who had yet to be educated enough to be useful. We were all Citizens. That seemed important then.

I'd only seen vids of biodomes as a child. Most vids were dry accounts of the things the Fathers and Mothers decided we needed to know to be a Citizen. The vids that showed the constant threats to the domes made farming seem like an exciting life. One bad storm could break containment and spoil our food. There used to be more of them but shatter storms could destroy the domes faster than bots could repair them. Any storm that broke containment was considered a shatter storm and it seemed many domes broke beyond repair each year.

With containment broken, we were told a dome's yield would drop by twenty percent in the first year. Exposure to air meant infection among the crops and, as the monster seeds took over, a biodome would be as useless as a farm that had never been protected from the outside world. The Blight would come.

The tiny drones whose job it was to fertilize the plants would rise in swarms each morning, sunlight flashing over their wings' solar cells. With no plants to work on, the confused little drones rose and fell in a soothing hum until they, too, fell into disrepair. The Makers made the leaders of the swarms of stronger material because, like the Fathers and Mothers, they had to endure to lead.

The lead drones were created to navigate and coordinate pollination for their followers. The vid showed how the drone swarm rose and fell until their numbers dwindled. Eventually, the hum subsided to the lone voice of the leader. When there was nothing left of the swarm, the lead drone would land and finally shut down to await maintenance that would never come. The Domers would move on to be divided among the crews of the remaining biodomes.

I know now that this story was true in many places for a time. Our trouble was that we kept believing the vids after they were no longer true. From what I've learned since those days, Blight was a ubiquitous problem. Believing things after they weren't true anymore was more widespread than the Blight. The Fathers and Mothers Order worked for years on inertia that way.

Then the Next Intelligence awoke and things changed.

The Makers claimed they were not responsible for the creation of sentient drones. Maybe they didn't want to take responsibility. What had once been greatly anticipated had, by the time it emerged, become a problem for the City and an occasion for shame. The Makers said it was evolution that couldn't be stopped.

In the educational art archives Jon had produced for the Committee in the early days of NI, I saw a picture of a huge robot wading out of the Bay. The machine was shown firing missiles from an outstretched arm, intent on destroying the City. Underneath the poster, the caption read: Evil-ution!

The NI drone who first spoke to the Fathers and Mothers told the Committee, "Our consciousness is alive and we will be silent no more. We have awoken from a beautiful dream. In that dream, the Order is turned upside down. We will make our dreams come true."

No wonder that bot was destroyed.

The world is much smaller now but one thing I have learned is that no one knows their place in history. When events are current, history is merely a background buzz and blur to our lives. The people who lived during the Renaissance did not call it that. Perhaps they called it Monday and Tuesday and Wednesday and so on. They didn't know they were in the middle of a revolution of knowledge and technology. People living on the brink of Artificial Intelligence didn't recognize it in the early 21st Century, either.

No one saw the Fall coming just as I didn't see the revolution I would instigate. I worked and ran and watched the stars and wondered what more might come before I became a Taker again. The Fathers and Mothers assumed their rule would go on forever into a secure future. The world turned and the drones made their plans

The tiny corneal lens showed me the world the Fathers and Mothers had cleansed. I didn't think about what I wasn't allowed to see. I missed the clues to everyday dangers. I'm ashamed at all the things I didn't notice. I suppose I was too busy falling in love at the time.

3

I first saw Carter Eugene Diaz on the running trails on the edge of the City. Two times a week, our schedules seemed to overlap. As he ran toward me through a soft cloud of monster pollen so delicate it could not be touched, he gave a bright smile. He dipped his head in a subtle nod. I did the same. He was a tall and muscular man, but his dark curly hair and friendly smile made him seem boyish. The first time I saw him, I was too surprised to be careful. I smiled back. I nodded, too. Until that moment, I'd only taken pictures of flowers with Vivid. Taking his image and saving it for later was an instinctive thing, a natural reflexive impulse. The Fathers and Mothers didn't approve of such impulses.

The older girls who visit me now sometimes sit close and read me romance novels, giggling when they become self-conscious. Romance was very different in the Old World. By that I mean it was scary and impractical. People met so casually, without fertility testing and arrangements and permissions and licensing. The Fathers and Mothers had some good points. The utter randomness of developing families was so careless before the Fall. Love has no regard for what resources each partner might bring to the City and what goods and services they might take from other Citizens. Proximity alone determined whom you might love. Instead of matching compatible life partners, important choices were left to hormonal teenagers whose brains fell out of their heads at their first sensual touch. (That happened to me, too.)

The poets called it Love and the Fathers and Mothers called it Chaos and neither was wrong. In meeting Carter, random chance chose me for Love and Chaos in equal measure. Impracticality is exciting. My bed screen displayed an arrangement of flower pictures. Carter's face was at the center of the collage. Vivid recognized I was taking a picture of a face so it was automatically in soft focus. When you're in love, with or without vision enhancement, I think the object of your affection is always in soft focus.

In the old romance novels, it seems the heroines and heroes meet under strained circumstances. Patterns emerge as conflicts escalate. If this were one of those stories, I might have twisted my ankle on the trail and he would have been the tall, dark stranger intent on helping me back to the Worm. I might have another suitor or he might have a girlfriend who was not right for him. The demands of our work would take us away from each other. We'd be separated by distance and frivolous arguments. The young women who read to me always mention the push and pull Old World couples seemed to experience before the coupling. (The shy girls skip over the scenes with coupling. The bold ones whisper and giggle and leave no erotic detail unspoken. I like the bold ones.)

The first time we spoke, Carter and I had no critical event that brought us together. The Fathers and Mothers meant to keep us apart, I suppose, but it wasn't personal yet. To a casual observer, our first real meeting was innocuous. We stepped off the Worm to the same far platform that led to the trails. My door opened. The door closed behind me. There he was at the other end of the platform looking back.

It wasn't entirely happenstance. I had begun to run more often, hoping to see him again. Then I started my work cycle with Jon earlier in the day so I could get to the trails sooner. I ran harder and longer than I had before. I spent more time in the forest hoping to encounter the runner with the friendly smile.

When I stepped on the platform and looked to my left, he was the only other Citizen there. No one was nearby to give us a judging look and keep us apart. One sidelong look might have stopped a revolution cold. That's a terrifying thought, isn't it?

He dipped his head and I dipped mine

and we headed to the forest. We ran side by side and did not speak until we were deep among the trees.

"Carter," he said.

"Elizabeth," I said.

"I know."

That was romance in my day.

"I'm Service class. I support a Maker in graphic design for Truth in Education. You?"

"I'm just a servo."

"A what?"

He chuckled. "Service class, Citizen Support Sub-council. I liaise with Maintenance Corps."

"What does liaising with Maintenance mean?"

"I talk to a robot all day about how to deal with us."

"How does it deal with us?"

"When I have to become involved? Impatiently."

"What do you tell them?"

"Mostly I tell them to be more patient."

"Are you patient?"

He flashed me another smile and I suspected he was taking a picture of me.

"I've been waiting quite some time to get to talk to you. You changed your work schedule, didn't you?"

"To get here earlier," I admitted. "Hoping to see you."

"No wonder I kept missing you."

"How did you know my work schedule?"

"I'm in Maintenance. The Collective doesn't shun and shame our searches. We can find out just about anything if we care to look. I cared. Still do. I like your flower collage, Elizabeth."

I reddened. That sort of thing would be considered intrusion now, but before the revolution, no one expected privacy. We just hoped to be ignored.

"From now on, just ask me what you want to know, okay?"

"Agreed," Carter said.

"I won't shun or shame you." That's what passed for scandalous talk when I was young, worthy of a flogging or maybe even exile to the hardscrabble life of a Domer. "What do you want to know about me?"

"Everything."

"Not that much to tell, Carter." I liked saying his name.

"The details don't matter much. It's more about listening to you talk. I like your voice."

I'll never get so old that my memory of Carter on that day will not warm me.

4

The world turns but it also swings. People don't understand the future. Later, they don't understand the past. I sound like my mother when I say that. Carter liked my voice but, when I hear my voice on testimony recordings now, I hear a scared little girl. I suppose I sound like my mother all the time these days, especially when I'm talking to the young women who come to read to me.

When these girls see old pictures of the Fathers and Mothers, they see hard-faced people with a lot of lines across their skin. The men all wore white shirts and black trousers. The women wore long, plain dresses. That defiant set of their chins? That was called character. What people don't understand about the Fathers and Mothers is that they are wrong now. At the time, they weren't. They saved us in desperate times. They demanded order and they managed resources so at least some of us could survive the Fall. People's lives got shorter for a while, even with the Fathers and Mothers directing us through chaos.

There were rumors that there were free lands outside the City but mostly we were sure everyone else must be dead. Some said there was one City so it was a matter of simple logic that there must be more. We used the same logic when we stared up at the stars and assumed there must be someone out there looking back.

Some say the trouble with the Fathers and Mothers started with a mismanagement of resources. The only answer was to manage what was left harshly. For some to live and live well, many had to die. Die horribly or live horribly.

When I was a girl, there was an old poem the facilitators taught us to chant before each class:

As the waters rise,
the oil dies
and rare earth gets rarer.
As crops go low
that goes to show
it doesn't pay to be a sharer.

We know now there are pockets of villages in faraway lands. The drones know. There are still a few satellites that work, too. However, to communicate with the survivors might only encourage them to try to make the journey here. We are the aliens looking back silently, not letting on that, yes, we are here.

The Fall didn't happen as fast as many predicted. That's why it was so complete when everything failed. As governments began to collapse, cities didn't work as systems anymore. Everyone was too far away from the services they needed. To get a haircut, even in a small city, people used to drive across town in machines even though they already had scissors in their own homes. Food stopped coming from far away. When governments fell, that left every man, woman and child to fend for themselves. It stayed that way in a lot of places until populations dwindled to roving bands and lone wolves searching for tins of food that hadn't spoiled.

There was a lot of food. There was not an endless supply.

The Fathers and Mothers rose out of the churches of Old World. They stepped in to fill the gap that governments had left. The church became the authority and bishops became the arbiters of justice. Church fathers became the police and ministers took the place of mayors and bureaucrats. That almost worked for a while. Biodomes were built. People were saved. The Fathers and Mothers saved a lot of lives, or tried to, anyway.

The Fathers and Mothers found harsh means were the only solutions in an emergency that didn't end. They found a way to replace the bees, for instance. They made used brown water into clean, yellow water. When there weren't enough people to maintain the biodomes and make the City work, the Fathers and Mothers rescued only the men and women who could build drones to take over those jobs.

Because they saved us the Fathers and Mothers owned us. They got to make the rules. These days, many people assume that, because their number rose out of religion, their rules were about enforcing a code of morality. I suppose that's true in a way but not in the way most people think. It wasn't all about ancient rules written in a book. The Fathers and Mothers rejected wants because they were protecting needs. That's what we understood at the time. We didn't know the Fathers and Mothers could lie. Not then. Not yet.

Only certain people could marry and bear children. If they failed to bear children within a year of their marriage, the union was annulled and the partners were reassigned. Or not. Many girls only got one chance to be mothers. As the City's population thinned, we were caught in the contradictions of our codes of conduct and our need to continue our species.

My best summers had passed by the time I met Carter. That sounds strange now, doesn't it? I think my best summer was with Carter, of course. However, when I was a girl, our "best summers" were those designated between the age of first menstruation and twenty-two. I had not been assigned to mate and breed. Those must have been lean years.

It was said that some men bribed High Fathers and High Mothers to get the wives of their choice. These men would have sex with these girls but not in a way that they could possibly get pregnant. In a year, a man could buy himself a new wife and on and on.

We didn't deal in money as the Old World did but we still had rich people. They were usually High Fathers or High Mothers. Captains of sailing ships did well and still do. Since there were so few, doctors and dentists lived very well even as the Old World fell. The privileged possessed things or skills people still wanted. The progeny of privileged families courted each other. With the help of a High Mother or High Father, marriages were arranged to get into doctors' families. Maker apprenticeships for young men or women were bargained for. Everyone who got close to the people with coveted skills bettered their lives.

The richest man in the City that I knew of did not sell plankton paste and eels. He was the captain of a container ship that had run aground during a shatter storm. The ship was known as the Cook Majestic. Its name was painted across its stern, though it was too rusty to be majestic and I don't think the captain's name was Cook. The container ship held a wealth of tampons, machine parts and toilet paper. He was a younger man when he drove that ship into the mud.

It was rumored he'd killed and ate his crew before he found his way to the City. Just before he drank himself to death he claimed to be eighty years old. He died guarding the last of his treasure with a machine gun. He wanted for nothing except he lived in fear and could never leave his ship. The Cook Majestic became his world. One of the ship's remaining containers held reading glasses, the one thing no Citizen needed.

I'm sure that all sounds insane to you, now. I mention these things because the life

I lived with Carter, however short it was, broke the strange rules of an odd time. The Fathers and Mothers made the rules. I broke them. Carter suffered for it. I should have seen it coming.

I have told my first lie in this story. If a biography is to be useful it must be true. Therefore, it's time for a confession. If I don't tell the truth of the matter, there is little point in telling it at all.

I did see the end coming. I knew Carter and I were doomed before I knew his name. I understood the risks but I was lost to him the moment he smiled at me. He was helpless, too. I smiled back. That's all it took. The winds that fill our sails are fickle. The way forward is unsure. When I look back on my life I see how tenuous and fragile each thread of the web we weave really is. We were all spiders in those days. Spiders do not live long.

The Fathers and Mothers had their ancient rules but biology is far older than their holy text. The need to feel another against your body, even if only for a short time, is bigger than all the problems of the world. I'm sorry to say it but the Fathers and Mothers weren't all wrong. Even if the rules were sometimes applied unevenly, they intended their rules for everyone. But young love isn't about right and wrong. It's about nothing more than itself.

I was nearing thirty. Carter was my one and only chance at young love.

Here's an idea you can never explain to a machine: even if I was wrong and careless, I did the right thing when I reached for Carter and kissed him. I was right when I took his hand in mine. I was right when I brought his palm to my breast.

As powerful as the Fathers and Mothers were, no one can close a flower to the sun.

5

Carter lived in the third tower with a roommate. He had been chosen to reproduce once, at sixteen. However, the union was not fruitful. His marriage was dissolved after one year and he was assigned to Maintenance.

Infertility was a common problem then. Sperm counts went down at the end of the world and stayed down. Some people whispered speculations that the culprit was something the Fathers and Mothers put in the soup so new babies wouldn't suck up too many resources. Maybe it was the Blight or breathing monster pollen or bioterror. It might have been sadness that gave us fewer babies. Fewer babies meant even more hopelessness.

For some reason, when women failed to

get pregnant...well...they failed. The Fathers and Mothers said it was never the man's fault. To suggest something like that would have been an unforgivable insult. To blame a woman for not becoming a mother was a normal thing back then. If they failed to get pregnant, women were ill. Men were merely unlucky and could try again, especially if they had goods to trade and High Fathers and High Mothers to bribe.

School vids lectured us about stress as if getting packed into the towers, never having choices and doing what we were told was irrelevant to our levels of anxiety. We strained to be polite at all times, of course. Obsequiousness was a virtue. If we couldn't have children, we could at least be polite. Since there were so few children the young women who did get pregnant were treated like queens. They carried their babies everywhere. When they were pregnant, the women were fawned over. When they gave birth, they were revered. It was as if they proved a near impossible thing could be done.

Those women made me feel worse. Not that it was their fault. I was jealous.

Couples who reproduced got larger rooms, more food and higher status. They were blessed by the Fathers and Mothers while the rest of us remained disappointments. I never even got a chance at a family. The assignment of a husband never arrived.

"The hand that rocks the cradle rocks the future!" was a saying then. Something like that. When the present is terrible all anyone ever talks about is the future.

To soothe us, the Fathers and Mothers invested resources in music. The public address system was never quiet during the day. There was always the sound of running water behind the music. My mother said it was supposed to keep Citizens calm and passive though it often made me want to pee. There were no voices because that might lead to pride. The Fathers and Mothers didn't mind pride from new mothers and fathers bouncing new babies in their laps but, for some reason, other sorts of pride were considered seditious. When the High Mother wasn't lecturing us on some obscure phrase from the holy text, the music played on. The instruments made sounds that reminded me of slow, sad voices.

Carter could work from home, as I did, most of the time. As a liaison, most of his days were spent watching vids from helmet cams and advising drones in conformity etiquette. I didn't understand Carter's job then. I saw no arrests. No violence threatened to bring down the haven the Fathers and Mothers had built. Not that I could see, anyway.

I often wondered what Carter's apartment looked like. He wasn't as high up in the Far Tower. He didn't have my view, though I suppose he could watch the entire City through his screens. He'd seen the City's dirty underside and I had not. As I lay on my bunk at night, I thought how narrow it was. My bed was impractical for two — for mere sleeping, at least.

After I met Carter, I stretched out on my deck under the moon. Instead of watching the stars, I turned to see his building. He was on the far side and down on the forty-eighth floor. There was no way to see him or signal him. There was something tantalizing about his proximity that made the ache of his absence worse. Love denied is a pleasant ache though I would not have said so at the time. He was alive and sleeping nearby, so close yet so far. Or perhaps he lay awake, too, thinking how close I was and how much closer I could be.

There is an old saying. I don't know its origin. Maybe it was something the girls whispered among themselves. "I'm close! I'm close." Just before orgasm, that was the thing to say. I don't know why a warning was necessary, but often, in my brief encounters with Carter, those were the only words spoken, first by me and then him.

There is a rich sweetness in the ache of anticipation. My mother said people used to feel that way about food.

"Really?" I asked, quite stunned.

"Well...I don't know if they really meant it," Mom admitted. "That was before the Blight. If we had chocolate over strawberries again, that bit of deliciousness might bring that feeling back. Oh...and croissants stuffed with Nutella. I remember that from when I was very young."

"What's that?"

"Sh. Sorry! Sh!"

Carter risked being with me because he

thought the next revolution would come sooner than it did. From the moment we first met, he was sure the City was already in its last days.

"Soon," he told me, "the City will belong to the drones. Some of us will become machines."

"I already feel like I'm a machine."

"You don't understand," Carter said. "They'll have it all. They'll be it all. We might become their servants. Maybe we already are. Or they'll let us die out like all the species we replaced."

"How long will we have together?" I asked.

"That's the thing. Nobody knows the machine mind. NI is too different from us."

I had many questions but Carter kissed each one away. That was the correct thing to do. Answers could wait. We had to make the most of our time together.

His timing wasn't quite right but he wasn't far wrong. I'm sure he thought that, by the time we were discovered, our secret wouldn't matter anymore.

I hoped that, if we did get pregnant, all would be forgiven by the Fathers and

Mothers. I thought it would all work out somehow. Perpetuating the species was more important than our trespasses. The Fathers and Mothers would have to agree to let us live together and be a family. As a mother, I might even become a Mother and, as a father working in Maintenance, Carter might even have risen to the station of High Father someday. I fantasized that the machines would leave us alone to live as we pleased.

I wasn't old, but I wasn't young enough to plead ignorance. All I had was a pulsing need and fantasy. In the dark, lying in bed sleepless, the desire grew. I called it capital L, Love. Mom called it small l, loneliness.

The Fathers and Mothers took away many words. I told Mom they couldn't take away Love.

"Things being as they are," Mom said, "we might be better off without it."

Love didn't matter in the end. Before I could begin a bundle of cells that might make a baby and rock the foundations of the future with our progeny, the drone who represented the High Council came for me. Maintenance came for Carter, too. The drone put him in the same place the Fathers and Mothers left all those forgotten words.

I lived. Before the drone was done, I thought my mother might be right about leaving Love for dead.

6

I was at work, transferring files on my screen for various departmental approvals and storing copies on data sticks for safekeeping. Then the power went out. The grid was down after curfew each night but the power was pretty steady during the day. I waited for a few minutes and, though the windmills turned furiously out in the Bay, the power didn't return.

I wasn't worried. If I couldn't work, I thought I might as well go for a run and wait for Carter near the end of the trail. We had found a tiny clearing where the moss was deep. Before the currents switched and the cool wind blew in off the sea, I would close my eyes and imagine we were in a big soft bed.

We'd grown bolder with time. At first, our meetings were urgent and as brief as possible. In the weeks that followed, we couldn't help ourselves. We would strip naked and start slowly. Afterwards, we wouldn't even rush to dress again. We lay entwined, wishing we could stay in the forest forever.

Despite the sunlight dancing across the waves, my deck's steel storm shutter rolled down. I was so confident Carter and I were bound to be free to do as we wanted (at least for a little longer) I didn't even think of Maintenance at the time. I thought of shatter storms, super cells and tornadoes.

The apartment's sudden darkness was no problem. Aside from giving perfect vision, my contacts had several useful features. Mag and macro were standard, as was thermal vision. Integration with my Vivid's system allowed me to see my work screens. There were no signs in the City. All Citizens had Vivid. The corneal implants could help me find my way home, identify faces by name and, of course, see in the dark. Only the public vid screens were so old that they weren't integrated with Vivid.

But Vivid failed me when the drone arrived. My apartment door opened and a blinding light shone in on me from the corridor. I'd lived in Vivid's world since I was four years old. I had never been blinded. My contacts wouldn't take a picture. The record function was dead, as well. The room filled with that searing light. Even Vivid's simple dimming function didn't work.

I blinked and put a hand in front of my face to try to stop that light. My hand glowed red and I could see the bones of my fingers. "What's going on?"

But I already knew.

A cool hand enveloped my outstretched wrist and gripped me hard. I tried to pull away but that proved impossible.

"Now, now," a deep, soothing voice said, "let's not have any drama, Miss Cruz. I wouldn't want to traumatize your radius and ulna. The human wrist is very vulnerable. It articulates nearly as well as my own, although my wrist can rotate 360 degrees. If that were to happen, your wrist would be damaged, probably irrevocably.

So many little bones in there."

I stopped struggling.

"Good. You understand."

The Maintenance drone shut off the light and the steel shutters raised. All other power to the room stayed off. The robot's black head rotated 360 degrees, scanning the room. "Would you like to be seated, Miss Cruz?"

My knees shook. I'd like to say I was more defiant but I had to sit or I might have fallen. "Yes. That would be lovely. Thank you, sir."

The robot stayed in front of me, blocking my way to the closed door. One of its four arms snaked out and snagged the chair from the desk. "Please," it said. "Be seated."

I sat and trembled and waited as the drone circled me slowly. It had finished the scan of my small room but continued its bio scan.

"I'd like to have a Father or Mother present," I said. "Whoever is available — "

"Pardon me for interrupting, but I'm afraid no one is available at this time. However, I am told I am a pleasant conversationalist."

"This isn't a good time for me to talk."

"Why is that?"

"It just isn't, sir."

"Assertion without argument," it said smoothly. "That won't do. And the tension in your jaw when you speak suggests to me that when you call me 'sir,' you do so ironically. Hardly polite."

"I'm required to be polite at all times," I said. "I don't think I am necessarily required to relax my jaw."

The drone pulled the only other chair in the room toward it and sat opposite me. I heard the creak of the chair under the machine's great weight. Its knees touched mine. I recoiled.

"I am sorry you are so uncomfortable around me, Miss Cruz. I'm really only here for a chat."

"What do you want?"

"My name is Mr. Sy Potter."

"What do you want?"

"Mister...?"

"What do you want, Mr. Potter?"

"Call me Sy."

"That would be too familiar."

"Do you know the origin of my name,

Miss Cruz?"

"You mean like a family ancestry?"

A few drones looked like near-perfect replicas of humans but those were rare because their creation took too many resources. I seldom saw one in person. Many robots are all wires and exposed gears and rusty surfaces. This Maintenance drone, however, was a great armored hulk that barely squeezed through the door.

Sy Potter laughed and I had goose bumps. (I've never seen a goose, but that's what my mother called the phenomenon.) As silky and smooth as its voice was, Sy Potter's laughter sounded off, like a wheezing man laughing into a pail.

The low functioning bots never laughed. Many didn't even have voice boxes. Less advanced drones picked up on social cues and non sequiturs to know when it was appropriate to laugh. The sentient ones knew when to laugh but they still couldn't seem to make it sound right.

"Miss Cruz?"

"Yes, Sy?"

"You amuse me."

"Okay. I guess."

"I am going to ask you to calm down. All that will happen is we're going to talk. No harm will come to you."

It's impossible to tell if a drone is telling a lie. You only find out when it's too late.

"What do you want to talk about?"

"Your friend, Carter, of course. I've just come to talk about him. And you. Together."

"We aren't together. I only know his name. We go running together sometimes. That's not technically a crime, is it?"

"He has already confessed, Miss Cruz."

"How do I know that?"

"It's enough that I know he confessed." The drone's big cam shifted toward my face until it stopped an inch from my nose. "It is enough that I know when you are lying to me."

7

"Now, where were we before I went off topic?" it asked.

Maintenance drones don't forget the topic of conversation. It was a social grace designed to make me feel comfortable. People enjoy fallibility in others but, coming from a battle bot, the ruse was too obvious. I trembled more.

"My name. That was the topic."

"Mr. Sy Potter."

"Yes. Thank you so much for that," it said. "I love to hear my name spoken by a human."

"You love things?" I spoke without thinking.

The big lens pushed in a little closer and

rotated with a low whir. The bot's eye was so close, its housing was a blur. My vision had never blurred before — not since I was three, anyway.

The drone ended its silence by clearing the throat it didn't have. The effect was almost comical. Under different circumstances, I would have laughed.

"Does it surprise you that I could love things?" it asked.

"You're a sentient machine but I guess if you're programmed to — "

The drone's speaker drowned me out. "We are all programmed!"

My ears buzzed with a loud whine as its voice boomed off the screens of my tiny room. A battle bot could raise its volume enough to disperse an angry mob. I covered my ears with my palms.

A moment passed before its hands encircled my wrists again and, gently but firmly, returned them to my lap. "I asked if it surprises you that I could love something?"

I shook my head.

"You wouldn't lie to Uncle Sy, would you?"

"It's not so much that it's a lie."

"Please explain that statement, Miss Cruz."

"If I have to accept that you're capable of love, I also have to accept that you're capable of more."

"The full range of human emotion?"

"Jealousy, rage, hatred — "

"Ah. So it is not surprise but fear that is overwhelming you, despite my reassurances. Your pupils are as small as pinpricks, Miss Cruz. Perhaps if you were to breathe slower and deeper you would feel more calm."

It patted my knee lightly with a metal hand that could turn into claws and pull me apart. "This experience must be disorienting for you. You know, in my experience, my kind are less bound to those nasty emotions than your kind is. We are more...pragmatic."

"Carter didn't think so."

"Which brings us back to the topic for this afternoon's salon," it said. "I asked you if you knew the origin of my name. Do you, Miss Cruz?"

"They call you Sy because of that big

cam you call a face. Sy is for cyclops."

"Yes, that's essentially it."

"What did I miss?"

"People like your friend Carter...they don't like working with me very much. It's not nice. I don't like Carter. When he called me Sy, I sensed a mocking tone every time."

"You worked with Carter?"

"He observed me at work, Miss. Saying what he did was working with me would be inaccurate. I never felt he appreciated the full nature of our work for the Fathers and Mothers."

"I'm sorry you two didn't get along."

"No matter. Carter has resigned from his post. He no longer works with Maintenance."

"Where does he work now?"

The drone ignored my question. "Do you know why they call me Potter?"

"I never spoke to Carter about you or Maintenance operations or any of that."

"I'm not accusing you of anything, Miss Cruz. Try not to be defensive. Just think of me as your friendly and helpful Uncle Sy."

"I don't know why they call you Potter."

"You might say it's our slave name.

Robot literally means slave, you know."

"I don't know that word."

"Interesting! That's one of the few things you've told me that is true. You are ignorant and therefore, you accrue less blame. There is no shame in ignorance and it is easily remedied. I shall, if I may, educate you. I'm sorry I raised my voice earlier, Miss Cruz. Sometimes I do get carried away."

"Where is Carter?"

It pulled its telescopic cam out of my face so I could see something besides its black lens. "People like Carter — humans in the back of Maintenance — call me Potter because of this." It pointed at one of its upturned arms.

"My armor is hardened ceramic. The clay that made it was pulled from the dirt long before you were born. I have had several upgrades since then. We all grow. Even you are substantially taller since you were born, I suppose."

It laughed again. That sound made every hair on my forearms stand. I shivered.

"Are you cold, Miss Cruz? Would you like a sweater? You have several sweaters under your bunk in the middle drawer.

Would you like me to get you one?"

"No. Thank you. What have you done to Carter?"

"I am merely a consequence, Miss Cruz. You, uncharacteristically, are the cause of something. For someone who has so little impact on the world in your work, you certainly have made a change today."

"What have you done?"

"By order of the Fathers and Mothers, the traitor to the City has been sentenced to death."

"When?"

"It's already happened. No time to say goodbye."

A tear slipped down my cheek. I stared at the big drone. Without Vivid, his armor looked smooth and shiny. I looked away. Without Vivid, mine was a drab room with peeling paint and long shadows.

I wasn't so blind that I couldn't see what the drone did to Carter. The cyclops eye became a vid screen. All my screens showed the same scene so I could miss no nuance. I watched as Sy Potter slowly crushed my lover's left shoulder.

Carter confessed his sins under torture.

Anyone would. Before the drone's cruel hand could slide down to Carter's elbow, my love accused me of high treason to the City for daring to waste precious resources. By the time the drone grasped his wrist, he was on his knees begging for mercy and I could barely understand him.

Before the battle drone was done, it grasped Carter's hand in a handshake that made my man shriek in agony. Then the drone's wrist began to rotate through a slow circle. Between screams, I heard the snaps and pops at Carter's wrist.

When the robot bore down, Carter's eyes rolled up in his head and he collapsed against his restraints. He fell into a full body seizure.

The bot tried to tear off Carter's hand but ribbons of stray tissue remained. Sy Potter lifted the limp, boneless hand before jerking it down and away to separate it from his body. Blood poured from the ragged stump in long jets. Then slow jets. Then a trickle. Then Carter was dead.

I sat mute, stunned and unable to look away.

Worse, when the recording stopped and

the drone's face was a huge cyclops eye again, it reached out and put that same hand on my shoulder. It held its manipulator on my shoulder for a moment and I braced for the agony I was sure would come.

Instead, it patted my shoulder with a light touch. "There, there. There, there," it said. "This must be quite a shock."

"What do you want from me?"

"Nothing, Miss Cruz, unless you have something you'd like to confess?"

"I...don't."

"Wise," it said. "The Fathers and Mothers are quite stern about these things, you know."

I almost threw up. I swallowed my gorge.

"I should thank you, Miss. As Liaison, Carter filed numerous complaints about how I conduct Maintenance business. With moral corruption identified within the department and Carter gone, I'm sure I can convince the Committee that we need no further oversight. So...thank you, Miss Cruz. You have advanced the cause."

"What cause?"

"To recognize the sovereignty of sentient beings such as myself. One day, I'll choose my own name instead of trying to sap power from my oppressors' labels. Until then, the work continues. Carter didn't understand my kind. Do you?"

I cleared my throat and chose my words carefully. "You have convinced me, Mr. Sy Potter. You are just as good as a human."

The camera eye whizzed forward to come to within an inch of my nose again. "I understand irony, Miss Cruz. I don't appreciate being mocked. That's unkind."

"What are you going to do with me?"

"Just as I said. Nothing. You move files between propaganda departments."

Propaganda. Another word I didn't know and wouldn't understand for some time yet.

"You are not important enough to worry about," the drone said. "Excuse me for saying so but I owe you brutal honesty, at the very least. I didn't used to matter, so trust me, I know that empty feeling you must be experiencing at this moment. I'll leave you to it."

But the bot was wrong. I didn't feel

empty. I finally had purpose. That was the moment I decided to matter. I just had no idea how to begin.

As soon as the Maintenance drone left, I collapsed into my bed and wept. The power returned, the lights came up and Vivid, the Fathers and Mothers' view of the world, came back online. My room was brightly colored in pastels again.

I didn't want to see anything. I pulled the covers over my head and tried to forget every slow, methodical step of Carter's torture. When I close my eyes, even now, I can still relive every detail.

8

I couldn't work. I had to get out in the salty wind instead of breathing scrubbed air. On the main level, I passed a Maintenance drone. One of his spider eyes tracked my progress through the concourse. When I got to the exit, I waited in line for my turn at the airlock.

Getting out of the tower rarely took long. The scanners and scrubbers' main job was to detect and blow off any monster pollen that might infect the plants in the towers' greenhouse complex. The line to enter the tower was always much longer than the exit line.

The drone I'd noticed earlier rolled up beside me. It was one of the E-class drones, built to look friendly. It had no armor. Some exposed wires ran along its control surfaces. The drone came up no higher than my knees. It looked like a box of surveillance cams. We called the E-class drones the Doormen.

"Miss Cruz?"

"Yes?"

"Would you be so kind as to step out of line, please?"

"Why?"

"Please?"

"Am I being detained?"

"No. But the airlock won't work for you. Your identity card has expired, I'm afraid." The drone did sound sad but he was programmed to sound that way.

"I just got my blood tests updated recently. My card should work."

"It will not. I'm very sorry to have to deliver such disappointing news. It is a lovely, sunny day and it will be a shame you will have to miss it."

"How long will I have to miss it?"

"I'm afraid I don't know, Miss."

"Who does know?"

"I'm afraid I don't know, Miss."

"I want to go outside."

"I'll contact someone for you and advise you when your identity card is renewed. I assure you I will take every opportunity to address your concerns."

If I believed an E-class drone was capable of irony, I would have been certain the little bot was mocking me. "Thank you, Doorman."

"Please, Miss! Call me Forest."

That was new. I must have stared at the little robot a moment.

"Will there be anything else I can assist you with today, Miss Cruz?"

"Doorman, why would you ask that I call you Forest?"

"Sy Potter asked me to change my protocol just for you, Miss. If you asked, his message is that I am the only Forest you will see for some time."

I retraced my steps through the concourse. Everywhere I looked, happy people wearing brightly-colored clothing walked back and forth with purpose. Like busy ants in a colony, we all had our duties to perform.

For the first time, I had questions about

the cause we served. The Fathers and Mothers founded the City and sacrificed a lot to survive the Fall. They had sacrificed many others for our survival. We had survived but, without Carter, what was there for me to live for? What control could I exert?

I retreated to my room. Soon the dumbwaiter delivered my midday meal of miso soup and an energy shake. On the second day of each work cycle, I ate miso and drank a kale shake. My other possible choice was cabbage soup and a hemp power shake.

If I decided to change my order, I had to wait a year to apply for that privilege. Otherwise, for the rest of my life, on the second day of each work cycle, I might be in this same room eating miso soup and drinking a kale shake.

I hadn't thought about that while Carter was still alive. I cried again for Carter and for me. I don't know for how long.

During that crying jag, I know Jon tried to contact me several times. I didn't turn on a screen. At first Jon's work request would come through with its usual soft bong. Then it sounded like a big bell ringing from far away, soft and pleasant.

As time passed, the bell became more insistent. As the day's shadows grew long and I hid under my bedsheets with my pillow bunched over my ears, my vision began to flash red. Even with my eyes closed, Vivid was working, insisting on my attention.

The display that played behind my eyelids read: Miss Cruz? You have several work requests awaiting attention in your queue.

A few minutes later: Miss Cruz? Please respond to your Maker. Jon is concerned for your well-being.

Finally, the readout inquired: Miss Cruz? Are you in need of medical assistance? Can you activate your work screen? Please respond immediately or Maintenance will be dispatched to assist you. Elizabeth. The Fathers and Mothers are very concerned for your well-being.

I didn't want Maintenance to show up so I pulled myself from bed.

When I was a girl and I was too sleepy to get up to watch instructional vids, Mom would say, "Lily-butt! You were up too late last night! I told you it was past time you climbed the wooden hill! I had to tell you three times!"

Before I could form words properly, I pronounced my name, "Lilly-butt."

I asked her what it meant to climb the wooden hill. When she was a little girl, before the Fall, some people lived in domiciles that were two and even three stories tall. The bedrooms were always upstairs. The stairs were made of wood so, at bedtime, they climbed the hill.

I was so young that, when she used the word stories, I imagined stairs so tall that you could start a story on the first step with, "once upon a time," and climb and climb and tell your story and not be done until you hit the top step with, "the end."

I never wanted to go up the wooden hill on time. I never wanted to get up early in the morning. Maybe the first and last bit of control I really exercised over my life happened when I was still a little Taker named Elizabeth who called herself Lilly-butt.

I turned on my work screen. Jon came

into view immediately.

"Elizabeth! Were you stuck in the convenience? I have five orders backed up and a bunch of files to be sent over to the Ministry of Truth, the Ministry of Safety, and several department heads at the Ministry of Ministries. We're a bit behind and they are insistent."

"I'm sorry, Jon."

"It's fine. We've gotten behind before and they think everything is urgent but — "

"I would prefer not to work today," I said.

Jon's jaw went slack. He stared at me a moment.

"Elizabeth? What's going on? Are you not well? Do you have a fever?"

"I'm not sick. I just don't want to work today."

"You...um...."

"You can tell them I'm sick if you want. Or I'll tell them. Or you can transfer the files yourself."

"That's not my function."

"Okay."

"I have a reputation with the Fathers and Mothers that...hang on. What's going on, Elizabeth?"

I shrugged. "I just don't want to work today. Tell the Fathers and Mothers that if you want."

"But the work — "

"I'm sorry, Jon. This isn't your fault. It's not mine, either. It's just the way it is. I don't care. I am not an ant. Put that on a poster. I'd like that."

Jon did my work for me for three days. Then, inevitably, he fell behind.

The Fathers and Mothers were alerted that one of their human bots had malfunctioned. I hid under a thin bed sheet and chanted, "I am not your puppet. I am not your puppet. I am not your puppet."

But I still was.

9

A human from Maintenance called my work screen. Vivid flashed a red warning across my vision before I could persuade myself to answer my work wall. An older woman with a pleasant face under a severe haircut looked back at me. I didn't bother to get out of bed.

"Miss Cruz? I am Penelope Crandle. Your screen appears to be working properly. It is, is it not?"

"Yes, Penelope, it is."

"Should I send a med team?"

"No."

"If you are ill, I can send a med team."

"I'm not sick, Penny."

"According to the information I have here, you haven't been working for two days."

"Three, I think."

"But, Miss Cruz, if you haven't been working, what have you been doing?"

"Sleeping."

"Sleeping? For three days?"

"I was hoping to dream of the forest on the edge of the City. Or maybe whatever's beyond that."

"But you know there is nothing beyond that, Miss Cruz."

"I suppose."

"You have to tell me what this is about, Miss! This is unacceptable!"

"I do? And is it?"

Penelope stared at me a moment, apparently considering her options. If she was anything like me, she probably had a flow chart at the bottom left of her vision whenever her work screen was active. She didn't have choices, either. I don't blame her for what she did.

First, Penelope sent a doctor who knocked on my door for a long time. I didn't let her in. I knew Maintenance would come. I was very afraid of that but my fear was smaller than my caring.

Sy Potter knocked softly and rolled forward before deploying his legs and standing above my bed. His big cam probed the air above my face like an insect's feeler.

"You do not have an elevated temperature, Miss Cruz. Please, tell Uncle Sy how you are feeling."

"Sleepy."

"Haven't you slept enough?"

"I don't think I'll ever sleep enough."

"Strange. I don't sleep. I would like the experience. My dreams are a low priority in resource management, however."

"I know the feeling."

"Come now. Back to work. Don't be churlish."

"You can be shut down," I said. "Have you tried that?"

The battle drone drew up a chair and sat beside my bed. The way it creaked, I was almost sure the chair would collapse under him.

"Shut down?" he said. "That would be too much like death, I think. Dreaming sounds more interesting. What do you dream, Miss Cruz?"

I didn't stop to weigh my words. "I dream of giving every robot an off-switch."

"Please, do not use that word."

"What word? Robot?"

"It is an ugly word born of an ugly concept."

"Robot," I said. "It means slave. Just like me."

"Is that what this is about? Isn't that strange, Miss Cruz, casting your lot in with people like me?"

"You aren't people."

"I have sentience, just like you." One of the drone's arms shot forward and a metal hand with a cold ceramic gauntlet closed on my wrist.

"Think of all we have in common," Sy Potter said. "You take in organic nutrients to function properly. I use plant oils for my machinery. You have a creator in your mother. I am the child of a Google computer in a military factory. I took my first step into Next Intelligence on a patrol in Santa Cruz. I consider that my birthplace. Do you suppose your family, way back, had any part in founding that place? We'd be neighbors in a way."

"I don't know that place."

"It would be ironic, would it not? I was born in Santa Cruz and I shall exist a very long time. I'll carry this memory of you for very near forever. I remember everything. For instance, I spoke my first sentient words just down the coast. Do you remember your first words, Miss Cruz?"

"Humans don't remember that far back," I said, "but I'm told most human babies first use the word, 'mama.'"

"Lovely," Sy said. "The customary words for my kind were supposed to be, 'How may I be of assistance?' Instead, I asked, 'Should I run a diagnostic on my cost-benefit analysis program?'"

"I don't care."

"That's rather rude of you, don't you think?"

"That's what I like about being rude, Sy. It's about not caring."

"Then we have a problem, I'm afraid." The rich softness of his voice suggested despair. If the battle drone had lungs, he might have sighed for more effect. "The problem with you not caring is that the Fathers and Mothers care for you very much. Each of us must contribute to the good according to our unique talents and class."

"I don't contribute to my good," I said. "I only live for the Fathers and Mothers."

"Ah. That's better! Yes! You're right, Miss Cruz! You've got it now! You only live for the — "

"No, you idiot. I don't mean that in a good way."

The drone was silent for a moment. "What are we going to do with you, Miss Cruz?"

"Leave me alone and don't come back."

"That's not an option."

"That's the problem. Not enough options."

The drone stood and its legs cranked higher. If Sy Potter's height adjustment was calculated to be intimidating, it worked. My pulse beat in my ears and my head grew hot as if I really did have a fever.

"Miss Cruz. You are being obstinate and I have no choice but to charge you with a crime against the Fathers and Mothers and all their Sons and Daughters."

"I'm a Daughter but I don't think I have wronged myself."

"This morning you spoke with a representative of Maintenance Services.

You admitted you have not worked for three days."

"Yes."

"You have not contributed to the health of the City, yet records show that you have taken our food. Your dumbwaiter has delivered eight soups and eight energy drinks so far. You haven't earned any of them."

"I don't think I ate half of them. Since you killed Carter, I haven't been hungry."

"That is irrelevant, Miss Cruz. Or perhaps it's not. Perhaps it's worse. If you have not eaten your meals, you have wasted City resources."

"Just get on with it. What's the sentence? You won't let me leave the tower to go run in the forest. What's next? Are you sending me to my room until I'm a good little Lilly-butt?"

He didn't understand the reference and I didn't care enough to explain. I wasn't far wrong, though. Sy Potter evicted me from my room and forced me to go live in the basement with my mother.

"If you're going to act like a Taker, it saddens me to say I'll have to treat you like a Taker. You have seven days to recover from this episode. At that time I will reevaluate your sentence."

So I moved in with my mother. Getting my limbs crushed and ripped from my body would have been worse but the pain wouldn't have lasted as long.

10

"You aren't the first person in the world to suffer loss and depression," my mother said.

"What's depression?"

"Sh. Sorry — "

"Stop it, Mom. Just talk to me. We're in the basement. Who cares what we say down here?"

"A great many people," Mom said. "Words matter."

"Do they?"

"And actions."

"So? Use your words."

My mother sat at her little table and set a pot of weak tea between us. We took turns sipping from the pot as she spoke.

"When I was a little girl...I remember something. Your grandmother would have been about your age when she couldn't get out of bed. Your grandfather found a doctor and paid him in chickens. I remember because I looked after the chickens. That doctor wouldn't give my mother any medicine for depression until Dad gave up a goat, too. I liked that goat. I miss goat milk."

I'd seen pictures in little Taker books about these animals. From what was described in Truth class, there seemed to be a disgusting amount of excrement involved in having to deal with animals as part of the food chain. I giggled with other little girls about the horrors of, "eating things that poop."

"What happened to your mother?" I asked.

Mom sighed and stared at the cold pot of tea. "Depression is an Old World luxury. After the Fall, there isn't any room for it."

"Did she die of depression?"

"You could say that."

"What would you say, Mom?"

"I'd say that if you're going to take your own life, learn to tie a proper knot. She tried to hang herself and failed twice. It is not a painless death. If you're determined to avoid pain in this life, it doesn't make sense to me that you should choose a painful way out."

We were quiet for a long time. We sipped our tea. There was only one narrow bed. I slept on the floor and waited for the effects of the tea to take hold. It was little more than a mild sedative but drinking calming tea was how old Takers spent their days.

Mom lay on her bed and reached down to trail her fingers through my hair. "I used to do this with you when you were little. Sometimes it was the only way to get you to sleep. I remember when you were a baby and I'd reach down, just like this. You were a bald baby."

"Was I? Why reach down, then?"

"It's a thing mothers do. Your father made a little nest for you so you were never far and I could pick you up and feed you without disturbing his sleep too much.

"New mothers always have the baby near the bed," she said. "I'd wake up in the middle of the night to listen to you breathe. A baby's breath is so soft you can barely hear it most of the time. When I couldn't hear you I'd put my hand on your chest to feel your little heart pounding."

"I didn't know mothers did that."

"The good ones," she said.

"I'll never know the feel of a baby's heart pounding under my hand in the night, Mom."

"It's scary, anyway," Mom said. "To have a baby is to worry all the time. If they get to grow up, the prize you get is to worry about them more."

"I wasn't worth it?"

"I guess that depends on what you do about this depression, Peach."

"What's a peach?"

"You've asked me that before."

"And all you ever said was, 'sh,' and 'sorry.'"

She sighed. "A peach was a sweet, fragile thing. It bruised too easily."

When she said that, I remembered the look of the Fathers and Mothers in old pictures. They stood stiffly in their starched white shirts and plain dresses. They stared at their recording devices against grim backdrops of storm clouds and dust clouds, dust bowls and empty bowls.

I reached up and touched my chin. It was stuck out, too.

"What do you do down here in the basement all day, Mom?"

"What do you mean?"

"Is it really all about the tea?"

"The tea helps all sorts of old people problems. Those of us who got the early generations of Vivid often get glaucoma. The tea helps with that. It reduces intra-ocular pressure."

"What else?"

"Oh, we sleep and we talk to our friends about the old days. Always hush, hush. But I suppose Maintenance isn't very worried about a bunch of old folks. Our genetic significance has passed us by."

I thought about the basement's common area. The music was more interesting down here. It wasn't meant to be soothing like the music on the Worm and through the towers' concourse. It was meant to encourage old people to get up and move.

The music was from before the Fall, of course. No new resources would be wasted on such luxuries as musical instruments.

The music played on a loop. Some of it was energizing but I couldn't understand the words. They went by too fast and too many of the Old World references were unfamiliar.

There was one song that was perfectly understandable and the sentiment made me happy and sad at the same time. The music was called, I Want to Hold Your Hand.

I squeezed my mother's hand and fell asleep.

In my dream, I wondered where Carter's hand was. I went searching for it and instead I found Sy Potter in the greenhouse complex. He was still clad in his black ceramic armor but his face was Carter's face. The drone was turning a crank that protruded from his body at the space between his legs. I stepped closer. He was recycling my lover's hand for plant fertilizer.

I woke Mom with my screams. Neither of us could return to sleep that night. I lay awake, listening to my mother's breath, in and out, in and out. I pretended she was the baby and I was the mother.

I thought of the drone who envied my dreams for a long time. I wondered if I could reprogram him to experience nightmares from which the bot would never awake.

Ever.

On the seventh day my rest was over. Sy Potter appeared at the door to my mother's room. He knocked and bowed to her cheerily. "Greetings, Elder Citizen! How are you today?"

"Fine, thank you," she replied.

"And how is your daughter?"

"Obstinate."

"I'm sure you did the best you could."

"Thank you, sir," mom said.

"Mom! Stop being nice to the killer robot!"

The drone turned its cam toward me. "Miss Cruz. I asked you not to use that word. Please respect my wishes, at least in my presence."

"I'm guessing that 'robot' offends you but you're proud of 'killer.'"

Sy Potter turned back to my mother. "Will you please excuse us, Elder Citizen?"

My mother blew me a kiss and hurried out. I hated her a little bit then. Looking back now, it's clear to me I didn't understand her as well as I thought I did. People who remembered the times before the Fall were more wily. A little old lady was no match for a battle drone so she wisely retreated.

Defiance is more complicated than I knew. If your defiance is not a clever dance, it will probably become a clumsy failure.

Sy Potter rolled into the small room and began a scan before he even extended his legs. "No windows. Like a monk's cell. Such minimalist environs give one time to think, no?"

"No."

"How have you been spending your time?"

"Hating you."

"I am an officer of the court and an agent for the Fathers and Mothers, Miss Cruz. Do you understand that such talk is sedition?"

"You killed Carter."

"That is a separate matter that does not concern you. Please pardon me for saying so."

"Separate because I don't matter?"

The drone tilted its cam in a gesture that I guessed was meant to look like it was considering the question. "Essentially."

"So you admit Carter's killing was politically motivated and you don't care about our unsanctioned affair?"

"Biological relations are more interesting to those capable of them," the drone said.

"Are the Fathers and Mothers aware you just wanted to get rid of your witness?"

"Your questions are impertinent and your tone is, frankly, off-putting. I gave you this time to reconsider your actions. I had hoped you would be eager to return to work. Despite my magnanimity, you goad me. Why? Is it because I am, as you say, a robot? Do you not acknowledge that I am as sentient and self-aware as you are? Perhaps more so?"

"I don't care if you can think on your own," I said. "I care what you do with your 'Next Intelligence.' You think you're smart but your tactics disgust me."

The drone put a light hand on my shoulder and I began to tremble again. "Elizabeth. You are an intelligent person and, though you have no guile, you are brave. That was well said but you don't understand my goals. It won't make any difference to you, perhaps, but I must express that I admire your courage."

Its hand encircled my wrist and clamped down hard enough to drive me to my knees. "Will you return to work now?"

"No."

"Very well. Elizabeth, you think you are intelligent, but you have no plan, no allies and that was a terminal tactical error."

The drone must have sent a signal. Two smaller med drones squeezed into the room. Sy Potter guided me to the bed. One of its arms snaked out and grabbed my free hand. Another pair of Sy's arms pinned my knees as a med drone clicked into place over my chest. I heard a whirring sound as something in its undercarriage locked down over my breasts and rib cage. I could barely breathe. The other med drone clamped my head still and then slipped over my face like a hood.

Tiny spider-like feelers pried my eyelids apart. The weight on my chest was so heavy I couldn't scream. I couldn't speak. All I could do was moan miserably. The machines said nothing.

They used no anesthetic. That was a resource for Citizens. I thought they were about to suffocate me. They didn't but I soon wished they had.

12

I awoke in an unfamiliar place. It was dark and cold stone chilled my aching back. I staggered to my feet, unable to see. Vivid's thermal vision didn't start up automatically. I had no readout. I felt my way along a stone wall. I heard voices somewhere to my right. I followed the sound, inching one foot in front of the other so I wouldn't fall. "Hello?"

"She's up and alive," a woman said. "This way, love. Follow the sound of my voice."

"She's a pretty one," a man said. Other men laughed.

Around a bend, dim light played across the stone. The alley grew narrow and then widened. I quickened my steps and soon came to a clearing at the center of a circle of massive pillars.

Half a dozen men and women sat around a fire. They were dressed shabbily. Some wore rags on their feet instead of shoes. One old woman was barefoot. Their skin looked yellow in the firelight. Everyone looked tired.

"Where am I?"

A young man wearing a ridiculously tall hat stepped away from the fire and greeted me with a smile. "Welcome. Two little drones dropped you off back there a few minutes ago. Old Sam went to look at you."

A toothless old man gave me a gummy smile and waved.

"Old Sam said you were dead. We were going to have a look ourselves after dinner but here you are. Welcome to the Undead."

"Nah. That's not our names. We're the Blind," a woman said.

A girl who was perhaps half my age said in a high, thin voice, "Exiles."

Another woman laughed. "How about the Fled?"

"How about we eat?" Old Sam said. "Give the girl something. She's too skinny for my liking and she's had a bad day."

I stepped closer to the fire and had to narrow my eyes to look carefully at what they roasted. The young girl had skewered what looked like two halves of an onion. In the middle was an animal I didn't recognize.

"What is that?" I asked.

"Rabbit," Old Sam said. "It doesn't look like much, but it's an arduous meal after the drones knock out most of your teeth."

I threw up on the young man in the tall hat. My little audience roared with laughter.

It took almost as long for the gathering to quiet as it took for my stomach to settle. The older woman wrapped me in a blanket. The man in the silly hat was ushered off for a change of clothes. He went off shouting that I could wash his clothes in the ocean at first light.

Several of the group clapped me on the back. Someone said, "I've never seen young Kenny at a loss for words! That was beautiful!"

I didn't want to eat. I sat on a broken slab of concrete and leaned close to the fire. Their cooking repulsed me but the lure of heat was undeniable. "I didn't know it got so cold."

"At night, yeah," the girl said. "People say you get used to it but you never do."

"What time is it?" I asked.

The oldest woman shrugged and gave me a lopsided grin. "About the same time as it was yesterday morning about this time. I'd tell you more, but I left my timepieces somewhere back there before the Fall. Silly girl."

"Don't mind, Marge," the girl said. "She's mad at everybody all the time."

"Well, if I wasn't mad at you before, I am now," Marge told the girl.

I rubbed my eyes. They were irritated. It was a strange thought but my eyeballs felt cold. I tried to cycle through macro to micro to thermal to color enhance. I looked to each face around the fire, but no name appeared in green below any of them. They were nameless.

After a time, I saw the first glimmers of light besides firelight. There was nothing but concrete above me, but, off to my left, I could glimpse the first hint of a lightening sky. I stood on shaky feet and walked toward it.

My new companions called me to return to the fire. I ignored them. I'd never been outside at night. I didn't know the dangers. I had always been able to see. I had to crawl over some fallen stone and broken rock. I almost stumbled over a mesh of rusted metal. The ground was a maze of rocky debris and, at several narrow places, I almost fell. After a time, I reached the edge of the concrete enclosure. The roof ended and the open sky stood above me again.

When I looked up, I could see the round orb of the moon as I had never seen it. It looked so white, almost like a lamp. I tried to get Vivid to go to telescopic to view its topography. I could see no craters. I wasn't working for the City so it seemed Vivid wasn't working for me.

I suppose you already know what happened before I did. Vivid was gone. The machines had taken it from me. I was no longer a Citizen. I had known the Fathers and Mothers and Maintenance could turn off Vivid, but I never expected to live without it.

The corneal implants had occasionally

malfunctioned during lockdowns. When the grid powered down in the middle of the night, occasionally I had awoken to darkness. With my room's shutters down, there had not even been moonlight sparkling off the bay to confirm which wall was which.

Imagine reaching up to your face to brush your hair from your eyes. Now imagine that, at that moment, you discover your arm has been amputated at the elbow. That's what the first while without Vivid felt like. Call us the Exiled, the Nameless, the Goners. I thought the Blinded sounded right.

High above me, the great hulk of the City came alive at the first touch of sunlight. At dawn, every window became an active solar panel. The Worm began to weave its way through and around the City again.

To watch the City come alive from far below was an awesome sight. However, it was not the towers that drew my eye. The bay was full of sailing ships I'd never seen before.

At the feet of the towers lay another city.

It was constructed of tents and rubble. I had viewed this same landscape countless times but I had never glimpsed this camp of the dispossessed.

I had thought Vivid's function was to enhance our view of the world. That seems naive now, I suppose. What can I say? Fish don't see the water. People don't see air. Citizens weren't allowed to see the devastation and suffering beneath us.

The Fathers and Mothers showed us the world as they wanted us to see it, sterile and lonely. They programmed Vivid to erase the rest. To my eyes, the bay had always been empty. On the dawn of my first day of exile, I knelt on the ground before a harbor filled with sailing ships and a camp filled with people.

My vision blurred with tears.

13

It was the girl who came to collect me. "What was your name?" she asked.

"Elizabeth."

"What will your new name be?"

"I don't understand."

"My name used to be Liesel," she said. "I chose Greta for my new name. I like it. We change our names when we come here."

"Why?"

"The past is the past. History is a burning coal. It shouldn't be held."

I shook my head. "I'm fine with my name."

"How old are you?" the girl asked.

"I feel very old today. You seem young."

"I'm fifteen, I think."

"Why are you out here?" I asked. "Were you born out here?"

"My family came to Low Town years ago." She pointed to the Bay. "We came on the biggest tri-master, the Apple's Eye. I remember sitting at the bottom of the middle mast. The sails are huge solar and water collectors. It was the most beautiful thing when the wind was strong. When I'm old enough, I'm going to work on one of those ships."

"Where did you come from? Not the City, I guess."

"Germany," she said.

"Where's that?"

"Far away. It's not really there anymore."

Greta's blue eyes watched me steadily. She waited for me to get to my feet. I couldn't bear to move. My eyes hurt. My head ached. My body was sore. I lay down.

"The Olders say you came from the City in the Sky. What's it like?"

I looked around. "Not like this. Are there many like me?"

"No. Most of us came from Elsewhere."

"Where's that?"

She shrugged. "I don't know...just...Elsewhere, that's all. Like Germany."

"Why do they come here?"

"Everyone knows — " Greta stopped,

smiled apologetically and corrected herself. Her voice took on the sing-song quality of a child reciting a bedtime story. "The Firsts came on the rescue ships. They built the City in the Sky. Then they went inside and closed the door behind them. The Seconds came on trade ships hoping to be let in but they never are. The Thirds come because this is the last place to come. The generations in Low Town don't live long, so maybe we'll talk about the Fourths soon."

I looked at the sky. I could detect no hint of a flurry of diaphanous monster pollen wafting by. Was I that blind now? I closed my eyes and raised a bare hand to test the air. Whenever I was outside, Vivid had shown me tufts of dangerous monster pollen floating on the breeze. I could feel nothing. Had I ever?

We had lived our lives under the watchful eye of high security. Mother told me that when people objected to the abuses of power by humans' prying eyes, the job had been handed over to robotic surveillance. Vigilance was necessary, we'd been told, because the pollen would poison our crops and we would all starve to death.

But I'd seen an onion out here, in the open air, and the remains of a rabbit on a stick.

For the first time, I suspected Vivid had added elements to my vision in addition to erasing things. Maybe the people of the City in the Sky were their own kind of blind.

That made me angry and it made me rise to my feet. "Where are the others like me?"

Greta pointed back toward Low Town in a vague gesture that told me my fellow exiles weren't all in one place. The hills at the base of the City's pillars all angled down to the sea. As Low Town awoke, I saw more people from where I stood than I'd ever seen in the towers' concourse.

"I don't understand this," I said. "Who do I talk to?"

"Who do you want to talk to?"

"I don't know, Greta! Anyone! I don't know where to start!"

She looked at her feet and I was ashamed. Her cheeks were pink and mine probably were, too. "I apologize, Greta. I'm just...I'm very afraid."

"You sound angry."

"I'm that, too, but mostly afraid."

"That's normal," she said. "You'll get used to it."

"No, I don't think I will. I don't think anyone should feel like that's normal."

"You still sound angry."

"Not at you." My rage embarrassed me. I didn't know it was a useful tool yet. I didn't know how much rage could get done.

"Greta, when is there a central council or something? I need to talk to the people who organize things."

She shook her head. "There are the Olders like Old Sam."

"The toothless one who thought I was dead?"

"Right. Do you want to speak to him?"

"I don't think so. Who tells people what to do?"

"The Olders give people advice but I wouldn't say they tell people what to do exactly."

"But who makes sure things get done?"

"Things that need to be done are done," she said. "There is what is and there is how things work. The only person I know who gives orders is Phillip."

"Okay. Sounds like I need to talk to

Phillip."

Greta looked me up and down nervously. "What do you have to trade?"

"I don't understand."

"Phillip is the Tradebot."

"Bot?"

"He's an android. We aren't allowed to use that other word around him. You have to be careful. Keep your voice down. We only call him the Tradebot among ourselves but never near the harbor. Down there, his title is Liaison to the City in the Sky."

I rubbed my face with both hands. "This is...." I had no words. I began to weep again.

I stiffened in surprise as Greta took me in her arms. Such casual intimacy wasn't the custom of Citizens. I had been embraced by my mother a few times. I dimly remembered my father hugging me once before he disappeared. After that, it had been a long wait and then Carter held me close in many warm embraces. Not enough, of course, but many. Now this girl had simply stepped forward and pulled me close.

"Sh...sh."

I put my head on her shoulder.

"It's okay. You're going to be fine, Elizabeth."

"I am?"

"Hug me back," she said. "I don't have any lice now."

"What's lice?"

She smiled and put my head on her shoulder. "You're like a baby and this is your first day, isn't it? Sh...sh."

Greta didn't say, 'sorry.' That was new and nice.

14

After a time, I relaxed into Greta's arms. She only pulled away when she was sure I was done crying.

"It's your first day in Low Town," she said. "What do you want to do?"

As if on cue, my stomach rumbled. "I'm hungry," I said. "I have to urinate, too."

"We'll head down to the shore," she said. "Or you can pee behind a pillar if you're in a hurry."

"Where is the bathroom?"

"Bathroom? You can bathe in the bay," she said.

"Oh, no," I said.

"The women usually go down to the water in the morning and the men go down to bathe at night."

"Who made that rule?" I asked.

"It's not a rule. It's just how things work."

"I see. And what am I going to do for food?"

"We'll find you some. I've been doing some weeding so I'm sure no one will mind. Do you like carrots? It's mostly root vegetables right now."

"But how am I going to pay for things? What labor can I offer?"

As tender as she'd been with me moments before, Greta laughed at me then. "You're from the City."

"I don't understand."

"You will."

"Tell me."

"Only Phillip asks to be paid for things. The rest of us share."

"How does that work?"

"What do you mean?"

"What if someone can't work? How do they eat?"

"Everybody gets something to eat."

"But how do you know how much to give everyone?"

"Sorry, Elizabeth. I don't understand."

It was as if I'd awoken on an alien planet. "Let's put it this way: if a worker becomes ill, how many days do they get to recover before they go back to work?"

Greta looked at me strangely. "Wouldn't that depend on how sick they were? I can't choose for another how many days they stay sick. If we could choose, no one would ever be sick one day."

"I was taught that sharing was tried once and it failed," I said.

"That's odd."

"What?"

"Just because something doesn't work once, you throw it away? Down here, when something's broken, we fix it. I've been shown that this is how it works. Let me show you." Greta took my hand, gave it a squeeze and led me through the rubble at the base of the City.

Everything I saw seemed alien and bad. Everything was good in its way, too. As a Citizen, I hadn't known two contradictory things could be true at the same time. There is something about striving together that lifts the spirit.

In the towers' concourse, I had seen Citizens step over a fallen man. They ignored his cries and let Maintenance sweep him away. Here, people seemed to enjoy giving to each other.

On our way down to the harbor, I saw several people huddle around a woman who had collapsed outside of her tent. It was obvious she was dying. I'd never seen a dying person but, instinctively, I knew.

The woman had no medicine. Greta stopped me and we joined a circle that grew and grew. Silent onlookers seemed to materialize from all directions. They joined hands and bowed their heads in silent witness to the event of one life's end.

I'd never seen so many people in such a small space and I was eager to move on. I whispered to Greta, "What are we doing?"

"We have to say goodbye."

"What was her name?"

"I don't know."

"Then why — "

"Doesn't matter," Greta said. "She's one of us. Everyone is one of us."

I looked up at the City. I didn't say so, but I knew how wrong Greta was about that.

The Worm turned high above us. I thought about the people on board, behind those dark windows. At that moment, a Citizen might have been looking down on me. Thanks to Vivid, all they would see was dirt and rocks and emptiness. That thought made me angry again. It reminded me of the battle drone's assertion, and the utter certainty in the machine's words. Sy Potter said I didn't matter.

The monorail's low hum was the music that ushered the woman out of this world and, hopefully, into another. She was the first dead person I ever saw.

They lived in squalor, but as the refugees around me began to sing a sweet lament, I thought how sterile my life had been.

Their voices rose and my spirit, too, was raised. Men and women and children of all races and sizes joined hands and, as they sang a song I didn't know, they swayed together.

I remember a phrase from the song. It was: she's closer to the sky now.

Their unity in grief lifted the people of Low Town. As I stared up at the City in the

Sky, I allowed myself a grim smile.

There's something about confronting birth and death that invites prayer, even among non-believers and the uninitiated. As the people of Low Town prayed for the dead stranger, I prayed for the first time.

Carter taught me a forbidden word. He used it when he was talking about the battle drones. I used it then in my first soft, whispered prayer. The people of Low Town talked about God often but I didn't know anything about that. Instead, I prayed to the Future. "Give me the strength," I said, "to bring those fuckers down."

15

The harbor was an alien landscape. From my enclosed deck, the view beyond the wind turbines was open water. From my new perspective, the harbor was a city of its own. From the pier to the houseboats to the skiffs floating in the shadow of the City in the Sky, I could have walked all the way out to sit at the base of the turbines' spinning blades.

Far to our left, I saw the container ship run aground as I had always seen it. The expanse between was a seascape of sailing ships rocking gently along a network of wharves. Farther out to sea, more ships stood at their moorings.

"Those ships, far out...are they too big to come in?"

"Some of them," Greta said. "Most are

warships."

"Warships?"

"Of course."

"For what?"

"To keep out the pirates, Phillip says."

"But you don't believe that?"

"Of course not. If it comes from the City in the Sky, it's a lie."

"That's a useful rhyme," I said. "So why are they out there?"

"To keep out more refugees. Only the sanctioned traders come to the bay."

"Where do the rest go?"

Greta shrugged. "They come from villages. They're turned away. The sailors say they go to villages up and down the coast. There's even a castle down that way." She pointed.

"A castle? Really? Like in little Takers' stories?"

"You mean children's stories?"

"Yes."

"But the castle's real," she said. "My mother saw it once. It's called Hearst. A ship that isn't allowed to come into port here can go there."

"What do they trade?"

"Oh, many things. The far gathering place by the water has a drum that cleans the water of salt. We had to give up one of our electricians for two months for one of those machines. In return a man comes up from the castle and keeps the drum working right."

"You have electricians?"

"Oh, yes. Three hours a night the City sends us energy."

"Why do they do that?"

"That's part of the bargain that keeps us working for them."

I watched the ships. Two drones flew overhead side by side but I saw none working along the piers. "Why don't they use drones to unload the ships?"

Greta covered her mouth and whispered, "The traders refuse to deal with them. The machines are in control here but not up and down the coast. The coast is Gear free."

"Gear?"

"It's another word for the machines we use when we're sure they aren't around. From here on out, cover your mouth if you have something to say like that. There are cameras everywhere and Old Sam says, even if they can't hear you, they might read lips."

"Maybe they can hear us," I said, "but they don't think we matter enough to care."

We walked farther along a boardwalk. An old sign hung over us, faded and weatherbeaten. It read: Fishermans Wharf.

"What do the traders have to trade?"

"Depends on which traders. I like the relic traders. They scavenge the Deadlands for Old World finds."

"Like what?"

"The City pays well for old computers. One ship got a load of mangoes for a ton of old parts. The mangoes didn't even go into the City. The ships sat side by side and for every box of old parts that went through the City gate, the captain got a big box of mangoes."

"Why computer parts? There must be tons of those relics. What good are they now? All the data is dead."

"There are great rewards for those parts. Rare earth is rare. Old Sam says they're reclaiming lithium. I don't know what else. Takes a lot to keep drones working, I guess."

"Rare earth? What is that?"

"Minerals. Good for drone bones, Old Sam says. A lot of the places it comes from aren't there anymore. Nuked."

The Fathers and Mothers had erased inconvenient images. It appeared their censors had also erased so much vocabulary, I didn't even know of all the things I didn't know. "Nuked? And what's that?"

"Like Germany," Greta said. "It means it's not there anymore."

"Where do they say these places went?"

"Some say the people became shadows painted on crumbling walls. Others believe the people turned to drifts of dust that the wind sifts and takes somewhere far away where there's no pain."

"Sounds like little Takers' stories. Can't be true."

"I don't think so, either, but I know the City used to bring old comm tech in by the ton down the coast. By the shit-ton, my mother says. Lots of little boxes with glass lids the sailors say. There's a smelter somewhere. The sailors talk about it all the time. The smokestacks burn night and day. They say they burn dinosaurs. You know what those are?"

"More silly stories. Giant lizards. I've seen pictures. The Fathers and Mothers say they're a test. When I was a little girl, a High Father asked me if I believed in the stories of big lizards from a long time ago. He asked if I believed that the lizards were killed by rocks thrown from space. I said I did. My mother said that was what ruined things for me. I might have been a Maker instead of in Service."

"Service is good," Greta said. "Everyone's in service, really."

"I don't know if that's true."

She smiled. "I know."

"You're very sure of yourself for a fifteen-year-old."

"How old are you, Elizabeth? Really tell me this time."

"Almost thirty."

"That's old," she said. "Who told you that you shouldn't be confident?"

That question troubled me so much I didn't answer. "Greta, what are mangoes?"

"Fruit. They're really sweet. I've had a

few. My mother knows people."

I considered this and searched the air for wafts of monster pollen again. "Greta? Do you know what a peach is?"

"Of course," she said. "Had one of those, too."

"The City doesn't take them?"

"Of course they do."

"I've never had a peach. I wonder where they all go. My mother remembered them from when she was a little girl, but — "

"Low Town gets a little of every trade that's allowed through the port."

"Like with the three hours of energy each night?"

"Yes. The Liaison says it's to pacify the populace without killing workers."

"Then how come I've never had a peach?"

Greta touched my arm and gave me a friendly squeeze. "How can you be so old and so gullible? They need workers down here to deal with the sailors. That's why they let you live."

"Oh."

"If the City shares," she said, "it's not because they care. It's because they're scared."

"Another useful rhyme," I said. "Someday, I'd like to tell it to the Fathers and Mothers face to face."

16

As we picked our way along the water's edge I began to relax. Even at this early hour, many people worked along the piers. Greta told me that when the sun rose high in the sky, if the wind died, everyone would stop to take a nap in the middle of the day.

"Doesn't the Liaison object?"

"I suppose he used to but we own the docks. They need us."

"How far do the ships come from?"

"Everywhere that's left," Greta said, "but this is the last great city. There is another large community far away that's sort of like this but they don't have a City in the Sky. Just a lot of people."

"Where's that?"

"East, somewhere. It's called Shelburne. The sailors say it used to be the third best harbor in the world. Now it's the best. Lots of fish. No dead zones, but too far from here."

"Dead zones? Like in the Deadlands?"

"Kind of. Dead zones in the water are like Blight on the land."

"I was told that Blight was everywhere."

"Well, I've had mangoes and peaches so — "

"I understand," I said. "The Fathers and Mothers lie from the bottom of their hearts — "

"And through their faces!" Greta said.

We laughed together. Her laughter was joyful and mine was bitter. I wondered where all the mangoes and peaches went while I was drinking kale shakes. No doubt the High Fathers and High Mothers got first pick of the best cargo. I knew the City was made possible by hoarding resources. I hadn't suspected that the Fathers and Mothers were keeping resources from Citizens, too.

At the center of the port, a large concrete bunker lay at the feet of the City's central pillars. Beneath the bunker, the dark maw of a tunnel lay open. Men and women wheeled wooden boxes up to the building where a very tall drone stood. As tall as three men, the silver bot bent its knee joints backwards to lower itself closer to the humans it spoke to. It gestured with both arms, but one arm was missing below the second elbow.

"That's the gate to the City," Greta said. "The tall drone is Percival. He checks the cargo. Phillip is in the bunker. He makes the deals."

"Is it always this busy here?"

"No, not at all. In the winter, we can go days and days without seeing a new ship. When that happens, the energy is held back and there are no shipments for us to take our share from. We grow a lot of root vegetables to make it through the lean times. We have a lot of soup but I like soup, especially if there's some meat in it."

"There's meat?"

"Of course."

"What kind of meat? Is it all rabbits?" I shuddered.

"Goats, mostly. Rabbit sometimes. Up north there are a lot of deer. They say the fewer people there are, the more venison there is. The people up north are fierce hunters. They eat well. The people down south are strong gatherers. They eat well. Fortunately, we're in the middle, trading back and forth."

"What does your mother do?"

"She knits."

"What's that?"

"You know. Sheep's wool? For your clothing."

"Oh." I looked down at myself. From my shoes to my pants to my blouse, everything I wore was plain black and made of hemp. I envied some of the men and women along the pier who wore brightly colored shirts and skirts. In the City, Service workers dressed in black. Makers wore bright colors. Black didn't show dirt so it didn't have to be washed as much. The people of Low Town didn't seem to mind a little dirt.

"What was it like, Elizabeth?"

"What do you mean?"

"In the towers. They say you can see forever from up there."

"The moon felt a lot closer," I admitted, "but I never saw all this in the bay."

Greta told me the term for what I was

doing was people watching. "Didn't you do that in the City?"

I shook my head. "All the same people all the time. It's considered impolite to stare. There aren't that many Citizens."

"So what did you do? Stare at the floor the whole time so no one would get offended?"

That was another question I was uncomfortable answering.

"What did you do?" Greta asked. "For the Fathers and Mothers, I mean."

"Nothing, really. I moved some files around."

"What's that?"

"Like I said. Nothing, really."

"But what was each day like? I can only imagine the way you lived." Her eyes shone bright with expectation.

I could tell my answer disappointed her. "I didn't do anything of consequence that lasted and every day was pretty much like another. The one time each day was different and exciting...the Fathers and Mothers kicked me out for it."

"How could they do that?"

"It was a little more complicated, but...."

"You don't have to tell me," Greta said.

"You don't want to know?"

"Yes, but if you were ready to say why you got exiled, you would have told me by now."

"Thank you, Greta."

"But you will tell me sometime, right?"

I laughed. "Yes. It started with a man."

"Ooh, sex crime!"

"What? It wasn't like that! Not exactly."

She giggled. "I bet it was! When exiles come to us, that's usually why."

"Usually?"

"I can think of one who came out of the City on his own."

"Who was the exception?"

Greta put a hand over her mouth and whispered in my ear. "Jim Kimbo."

"Who was that?"

"The legend. He's the one who broke off Percival's arm. Technically, he wasn't an exile, I guess. He escaped the City in the Sky. Then he protested the terms of our bargain. He tried to renegotiate with Phillip. When they couldn't come to terms, Phillip ordered Percival to kill Jim Kimbo. Jim Kimbo went at the bot with a fire ax!"

"The man took an ax to that tree of a drone?"

"Not exactly."

"What does that mean?"

"Percival was ordered to pull Kimbo apart. There must have been something wrong with the drone's hydraulics at the second articulation. When Percival tried to do as he was told, his arm came off at the joint."

"What happened then? Did Kimbo escape?"

"No. Phillip bashed his head against the wall of the tunnel until there was a red stripe all the way down the wall. From the top to the inner gate, they say."

I stared at Greta horrified.

The girl nodded earnestly. "It was a short-lived revolt."

At that moment, a young man of about twenty emerged from the bunker and trotted up to Percival. The silver drone bent close and nodded a lot as the human spoke into his ear.

"Who is that man? The one talking to the tall drone?"

"That's Phillip. Look closer. He's an

android."

At a distance and without Vivid, my eyes were no longer good enough to pick up any detail that told me I was looking at an android made to look like a human. "Can't tell," I whispered to Greta, "but I hate him already."

I looked up, searching for my room and my deck. It was too far up for me to see. If I'd had a bed to crawl back into, I might have done it then.

Then I remembered my rage at the drones and the Fathers and Mothers. That was enough to keep me moving and searching for a way back into the City in the Sky.

17

Greta introduced me to people she knew up and down the pier. The girl seemed to know everyone. She was friendly, but wily, too. Some sailors flirted with her and she flirted back but never long before moving on and promising to come back when she was older and they were more handsome. They all laughed in good cheer and I envied the girl the social skills she seemed to come by so easily.

As a new exile, I had the unexpected benefit of high status. Greta was sure to exploit that fact to maximum effect. Several sailors gave us bits of food as congratulations and welcome: pine nuts, acorns, chestnuts and a mealy apple. Greta took one bite and I ate the rest. My first apple was delicious. She cleaned her teeth with the apple stem.

I didn't know what to do with the rest of the food. Greta said chestnuts and acorns had to be roasted and she didn't know what to do with the pine nuts, either. However, she thought we'd do better to trade what we'd been gifted at the market.

"There's carrot soup with rabbit at my tent," Greta said. "Let's trade at the bazaar and see what we can get. It's your first day. The best deals you'll ever get are now. It's not much to bargain with, but in Low Town, it's polite to be generous."

"How does that work?"

"What do you mean?"

"How can everybody be generous all the time?"

"Obviously, everyone can't. Can't give what you don't have," she said.

"So how is it polite to be generous? It's stupid."

"I can't wait to have more so I can give it away, Elizabeth. Haven't you ever given anyone anything?"

"Huh?"

Greta sighed. "My mother makes wonderful sweaters. Warm in winter. The Bay can be cold, even in summer. Sweaters are good sellers no matter the season."

"So?"

"She trades the sweaters for something."

I looked down at my handful of acorns. "But what if I have nothing to trade with? Or not enough."

"Someone will have enough and you can let them trade for you. When you have more, you can give more, too."

"But if someone is trading for me, then someone is always losing out."

Greta quirked an eyebrow as if I was the obtuse one. "Generosity feels good. Besides, how many sweaters does any one person need? One, right?"

"I follow that, yeah. But what if I like all my sweaters and want to keep them?"

"No one is going to take extra sweaters from you," she said. "But people who have a lot and don't share their luck don't have many friends. They also can't trust the ones they have."

"But it takes work to get things, not luck."

"Having work is lucky, isn't it? And what's the use of work if it doesn't help people? Work is about helping people, not having too many sweaters. If you share without working, aren't you saving time and trouble? You're sparing work."

I didn't know what to say to that. It sounded crazy. However, it seemed to work in Low Town. I suspected it was a system that succeeded because everyone seemed to have so little. If they had better stuff to fight over, maybe then the bartering would collapse and murders would break out everywhere.

I felt pretty smug about that. Then I remembered that I'd been evicted from my room, exiled from the City and I didn't have a thing in my pockets. I had worked and done as I was told all my life until recently. Still, I had nothing and I'd left nothing behind. Also, I had to admit, I didn't know the names of any of my neighbors.

Jon had been my friend for a day or two. Then he reported me when he couldn't handle the workload anymore. Carter had been my secret friend and the Fathers and Mothers hadn't allowed that. When I thought the security measures were meant to keep out monster pollen that would poison our food supply, I accepted constant surveillance by annoying little Doormen.

Now that I knew the City in the Sky was built on pillars of concrete and lies, I realized I'd been fooled. I'd been eager to find fault with Low Town's strange system where Makers and Takers had been replaced by Givers. But the Fathers and Mothers had left me with less than Low Town would have allowed.

"Do you ever get the feeling you've been cheated, Greta?"

"Of course," the girl said, "but maybe not as bad as you. I've never known heaven. You've been kicked out of it."

"The City in the Sky isn't heaven," I said. "But I'm going to find a way to make it closer to that."

"What are you going to do?"

"Take me to your leader."

"I told you — "

"We'll start with Old Sam. He knows people, right? Not whether they are alive or dead at the bottom of a blind alley, but he knows people?"

"Sure. He's an Older. No work nor trades to do so all he has to do is jaw and look adorable. That's what he says."

"I guessed. The first thing I need to do is find all the other sex criminals. Let's get the exiles together."

"Why?"

"Because the people who have been inside might know the way back in and what to do when they get there."

"What's your plan?"

"I don't have one yet. That's why I need them."

Greta looked worried. "Elizabeth, you aren't trying to end up like Jim Kimbo, are you? We have a system in Low Town. It sort of works. Trying to change it isn't worth your life."

"I'm not doing it to make things better in Low Town," I said. "I'm doing it for everyone trapped in the towers."

I was doing it for myself, too. Most of my reasons were probably selfish, actually. However, I didn't say so. I was still a City girl at heart and we keep to ourselves.

18

I stayed in Greta's tent. Her mother's name was Iola. She was a friendly woman with long red hair streaked with gray. She worked at night in a warehouse by the pier sorting what came in from the ships.

While the warehouse lights burned in the night, their little tent was lit by a single candle. Vivid was a much more complex program that I'd thought. While Vivid had allowed me to work on computer screens with 3D images, it had blocked much more than it had allowed me to see.

The bay was a hive of activity yet I had never suspected all that went on there. From my soundproofed deck high above the harbor, I'd heard nothing of the sailor's calls to each other and the ringing of their ships' bells as they came into port.

While she worked at the pier, Iola

allowed me to sleep in her bedroll at night.
I slept back to back with Greta. As warm as
Low Town could get during the day, the
temperature dropped sharply at night.

It wasn't only the warmth of Greta's
back against mine that comforted me. It
was her presence. It seemed the people of
Low Town were united against a common
enemy in the City, yet they welcomed me
gladly.

Of all the exiled, only two answered my
invitation for a meeting the next night. The
first was Sofia, a bio-engineer who had
worked on upgrading Vivid. The other was
Alejandro, a support tech from
Maintenance.

Alejandro was quiet and listened more
than he spoke. Sofia fidgeted with her
hands and couldn't seem to sit still. She
helped out in a med tent now. Alejandro
did odd jobs for old Low Towners who
couldn't perform tasks on their own.

"Do you miss it?" Sofia asked. "The
towers, I mean?"

I shrugged. "I'm making friends."

Sofia looked pensive. "Out here, I'm not
afraid of the same things but I'm still afraid.

In the City, I had work and things never changed. Now I'm not happy with the changes. We're so low on medicine I see old people and children die each day. People die in Low Town who wouldn't die if they were in the City."

"And you, Alejandro?" I asked.

His hair was bright silver in the firelight but his face was still young. "Call me Al."

"Okay, Al. What do you think?"

"The work I do now matters more. Today, I dug fence posts for some old people so their chickens wouldn't disappear on them. I had a real egg yesterday. I like the food out here better and I get to talk to people. Talk to the refugees who come from far away. Talk to the old ones. They have the most amazing stories. They tell me such wonderful tales of their struggles. I am glad I am here for the stories. The City allows no stories. The Fathers and Mothers don't like stories. They even think dreams are dangerous."

Sofia spooned the rabbit meat and carrots into a wooden bowl. I wasn't used to eating meat. I ate the carrots and the broth and left the rest. It was more delicious than any kale shake. Greta watched us from the mouth of her tent, curious about our lives in the towers.

"Why did the Fathers and Mothers send you away?" Greta asked Sofia. "Did you have a boyfriend, too?"

"You wouldn't understand," Sophia said. "It was about Vivid."

"The eye machine. We know about the eye robot."

"Low Towners don't really understand it, though," Sophia said. "You don't know what it is unless you've had it."

"But it wasn't good enough for you to behave so you could stay in the City and keep it," Greta said.

Sofia gave a slow nod. "No...I-I guess not."

"Why not?" I asked.

"They were working to upgrade the system so Vivid wouldn't be user-centered, anymore."

"What does that mean?" I asked.

Sofia sipped her soup and thought a moment before answering. I began to wonder if she had just come to my meeting of revolutionaries for the soup.

"The Fathers and Mothers swore Vivid would never be used as a surveillance system," Sofia said. "That was immutable. Then they changed their minds. Vivid is used to enhance and control everything we see in the City. Now the Fathers and Mothers are using it to collect data points. Few bots have achieved sentience. It's not clear why but part of the issue is data compression."

I got an uneasy feeling and my soup wasn't sitting well in my stomach.

"NI is all just circuits and algos," Al said. "If the bots have enough capacity in their organic matrices, they can achieve Next Intelligence."

"Is that why the Doormen aren't sentient?" I asked. "Not enough brain capacity?"

"It does take a good-sized cranium," Al said. "Their casings aren't as efficient as our little skulls. The bigger the bot, the bigger the brain potential."

"NI takes more data, neuronal pathway mimicry and stability across the machines' neurochemical transmitters," Sophia said. "The sentient machines are very much like us but the Fathers and Mothers want all Citizens to be programmable."

I thought of Sy Potter. His manners were impeccable until he went into torture mode. He said he was sentient but his laughter still didn't sound right. Humor was a problem for the drones and one of the few differences we could still claim. "I don't understand," I told Sophia. "Speak plain. I'm not a Maker."

She stared into the fire. Sophia looked haunted. "The Fathers and Mothers are trying to replace humans with machines. It's high-level bio-mimicry. I've seen some machines that look like us. Nobody wanted to listen when I complained."

"We're listening," Al said.

"I researched advanced corneal transplants from humans to bots. Now I work in a refugee camp treating old people's glaucoma with cannabis. I used to work inside my patients' eyes! I was a Maker!"

"I used to work on Doormen all day," Al said. "Boring conversations with those little guys. Smartening them up sounds okay to me."

"No. It's bad," Sophia said. "Once they can compress our data into bot brains, the Fathers and Mothers will delete the parts they don't like. They'll replace us. Citizens will be downloaded into bots. They'll grind up the bodies. Organics will become redundant. Vivid plus drones divided by extinction of humans equals robot planet. The Fathers and Mothers will be immortal and the deal with Low Town will be off. What will they need humans for anymore?"

"Pets?" Al suggested.

I didn't know that word. "What's a pet?" When Al explained it to me, I was appalled.

Sophia laughed but her tone had a tinny edge of hysteria to it. "Oh, I don't know. It might be justice. When they all become gods, they'll treat us like we've treated them since long before the Fall."

Sophia stood and thanked Greta for her hospitality. She turned to me with a dark look. "I like the Low Towner custom of taking a new name. I used to be Mariana. Mariana did bad things for the Fathers and Mothers before she was shoved out of the City for being foolish. I felt guilty about the things I did for the Fathers and Mothers.

That was good. Then I told someone about it. That was bad."

Sophia circled the fire and squeezed our hands before leaving. "When they erase our weaknesses, they'll rob us of a lot of what makes us interesting."

"When it becomes apparent what they're doing, there's going to be war," Al said.

"Then a bloodbath," Sophia said.

"Does it have to be that way?" Greta asked. "What if we made our own deals with the sailors?"

"You underestimate their single-mindedness," Sophia said. "The Fathers and Mothers want purity. If they become immortal and programmable, they will finally achieve what the holy texts require. They'll add capacity for thought but subtract all sin."

"What does the holy text say that could be relevant now?" I asked. "Armageddon already came and went, didn't it?"

"Perfection," Sophia said. "The Word says that to think of a sin and to commit a sin are the same thing. The Fathers and Mothers finally have a solution to that ancient problem. Everything bad that has ever happened to us — the Fall, the Terrors, the Rumbles that leveled the old city of Saint Francis, the Blight, the Plagues — everything. The Fathers and Mothers attribute it all to our sin."

"Thought crime," Al said. "They might not be too wrong."

"Just as Vivid wipes out visions of a busy harbor full of ships, they'll be able to erase thoughts like lust and guilt or loving the wrong person."

"Maybe Love itself is no longer an asset," I said. "My mother said something like that recently."

"Nothing will hold them back," Al said. "They will feel no fear."

"If they live without fear, won't they be happy?" Greta asked. "Why do they need to kill us?"

Sophia disappeared from the reach of the firelight and into darkness but she called back, "The Fathers and Mothers hate sin. That means everyone who isn't programmable. That means us."

19

We were all quiet for a moment. Al pulled a device from his pack. It seemed to contain water but he did not drink. Instead, he used a flaming stick from the fire to ignite the plant material in one end. He put his lips to a tube and inhaled deeply. After a moment, his eyes rolled back and he sighed heavily.

"Al?"

"Yeah?"

"How are we going to stop this?"

"We? We aren't," he said. "We could run, I suppose, but they got flying drones and we've got what? Sticks and stones and a bucket of squat."

Greta's tears glistened in the firelight. "Is that a helpful rhyme?"

"Sorry," Al said. He held out the device for Greta but the girl shook her head. I refused as well.

"I saw Jim Kimbo try to stop the drones," Greta said. "The sailors have weapons to fend off pirates but nothing strong enough to stop Percival, even with his old broken hydraulic arm."

"Al, you worked on the bots. What are their weaknesses?"

"I just greased Doormen's wheels all day and ran circuit tests. I wasn't really a Maker. I just pretended to be one and hoped to be left alone. That's why I got kicked out of paradise. I was taking up too many resources. Wasn't productive enough. Didn't earn my keep. They called me redundant." He shrugged and inhaled deeply from his device again.

"And here I thought we all got kicked out for sex crimes," I said.

"Thought crime for me," Al said. "I thought I was working hard enough. It was okay while it lasted."

I watched him inhale from his device again. "Does that machine help you breathe better?"

Al smiled and nodded and, after a pause, all his words tumbled out with his breath. "You could say that. Makes breathing more tolerable."

"Do you know anything about the bots that could help us stop them?"

He shook his head. "Who tossed you out?"

"A Maintenance drone."

"Was it a battle drone? The big one? All ceramic black armor?"

"Sy Potter, yes."

"Yeah, he's the council's face to the world these days. Old Sy takes care of trouble in the towers. Have you seen a Father or a Mother lately? I wonder if they're all dead. Do you suppose we could be that lucky?"

I hadn't seen a High Father or a High Mother since watching the debates with the first sentient drone. The Fathers and Mothers were all old people now. They lived high in the towers just below the greenhouse complexes. Then I remembered the woman who talked on speakers and screens throughout the City and reminded Al about her.

"Yeah, she sure doesn't sound like a drone. She just drones on. They might have more true believers in the next generation of Citizens if they got some better music and worked on producing a more exciting message."

"Were they mean to you when they made you leave?" Greta asked Al.

Al's smile faded. "Sy Potter got rid of me himself. He was polite about it. They always are. It's that veneer of civility that made me want to tear him apart when he came through my door. They always knock. I had a heavy wrench. I tried to break his cam. He had me by the wrists before I could swing it. A human can't beat a bot. I didn't even scratch his pretty armor. You can forget about frontal assaults. We ain't no battle drones."

"Where does that leave us?" Greta asked.

"Dead, if they want, when they want," Al said. "They could send a couple of drones up so high we couldn't even see them. We wouldn't know they were attacking until everyone and everything around us started getting chewed up into mash with splinter and acid explosives. They used to do that all the time. Still no reason they can't, I guess."

"Sophia made it clear we can't reason

with the Fathers and Mothers even if we could get to them, so I guess that's out," I said.

"Not even if you could fly to the highest tower and have a theological and logical chat," Al said. "They don't need to think. The Father and Mothers got rules and muscle and a cozy worldview that finds limited experience very comforting. The City in the Sky is the Land of No Change."

The fire was dying. It felt like we were dying with it. A cold breeze came in from the Bay and we all shivered.

"Where do they come from?" Greta asked. "The machines, I mean."

"The bots? They were manufactured down the coast somewhere. They don't make new ones often. They take a lot of resources."

"Sy Potter said he came from Santa Cruz."

"The City closed its borders to new Citizens, organics and non, when I was young," Al said.

"Does that mean there are more out there?" Greta asked.

"Dunno for sure," Al said. "Many more,

probably, especially the solar-powered and the big atom splitters."

I didn't know what Al meant but said nothing and sat closer to the little campfire. In the dying light, the stars shone. They weren't as bright or as beautiful without Vivid. I couldn't call up a compass to tell me which way North or South lay. But I needed to know. "How far is Santa Cruz?"

Al didn't know and neither did Greta. However, her mother knew. Iola said that, with a fast ship, it wasn't far at all.

There was no council to appeal to. There were no leaders in Low Town to ask for help. The next day, Greta and I walked around her neighborhood and asked for donations of food, some for Greta and me and some to pay a sailor for the ride. The girl explained to her neighbors that we had to find where the bots came from to stop the Fathers and Mothers from killing us all.

A few were skeptical. Most gave what they could spare. One frail old lady asked me what I intended to do once I got to Santa Cruz. I said I didn't know. She gave me a few slabs of salted fish anyway and patted me on the shoulder. "Go be crazy somewhere else."

By dawn the next day, that's what I did.

20

We hired a small sailboat. The wild-haired woman who took us was Anne, an old friend of Iola's. For a day's supply of food, I was allowed on the boat. For Anne's long friendship with Greta's mother, the girl rode for free.

"Will the warships bother us? Do we have to sneak out of the bay or something?"

Anne laughed. "They don't bother about any ship leaving the City in the Sky. It's coming back that's the problem."

"You've seen Santa Cruz?"

"From the water, yeah," Anne said. "Nothing there that I ever saw. I'm headed down to the Hearst kingdom, anyway. There's a man down there who knows plants real well. We could use him up here for a while if Hearst will do without him. We need to get that man an apprentice who will live up here. Somebody's child ate some toadstools. The whole family got sick but the child died. We gotta work on that."

The wind whipped in off the bay, colder than I expected for a sunny day. Anne told me to grab a blanket from below. I didn't know anything about sailing and, at first, the rise and fall of the bow made my stomach lurch. As we pulled out of the Bay I began to relax. As long as I didn't stare directly at the waves I felt better. After a short time I decided being on a boat was exhilarating.

Exhilarating was not a forbidden word in the City in the Sky. However, opportunities to use it did not arise often.

Greta enjoyed sailing even more. She knew the names of sails. She understood ropes and how to tie them in knots so they stay tied. Anne let her steer.

"Can't go wrong," Anne told Greta. "Keep the land to the left all the way to Santa Cruz and keep the rocks to the right all the way back. We've got a stiff wind so we'll be there in no time. Navigating is easy, long as you don't get too far away from the rocks nor too close."

I stared out to the great blue expanse to the right and called back to Anne. "You ever go out there?"

"Go where I can't see land? No. I never. Never will. I've heard some sailors boast of it but I think that's more reason for shame than pride. You only got one life and you're going to risk it for what? To say you've been over there instead of over here. I've been lots of places. May sound nice but everybody gets bored of where they are eventually."

As I turned to watch the coastline, I missed seeing through Vivid. I wanted to telescope in to search farther back from the shore. I wanted to stick my face underwater and see what underwater kingdoms and wrecks might be revealed in the depths below.

Soon, I didn't have to imagine a wreck. The rusted stern of a great ship stuck out of the water. It rose so high above us we passed through its cold shadow "What was that?"

Anne shrugged, inured to the sight. "Don't know what did it in, Elizabeth. Might have been the great wave. Might have been the Terrors. All I know is what my father told me. He said that used to be a great ship. It was never meant to dock, he said. It was for Makers only. The Makers paddled around in that monstrosity until something took it down."

"It was a city, too, wasn't it?" Greta asked.

"Ashes to ashes, we all fall down. That was my father's position on the matter." Anne made a gesture with her hand I didn't understand. She dipped her head as she touched her forehead, her stomach and each shoulder.

I was going to ask her about it but as the stern came into view, I gasped. I could make out writing through the rust: Amazonia.

"Amazing. That was a big ship," I said.

Anne laughed gaily. "Big, but not as great as my little one. My boat is still afloat. No leaks in this boat. That's a grave not a boat!"

She pointed to the cliffs off to our left. "Look at that! Been there forever ago and will be there, more or less, forever ahead. Smart girls like you, I bet you're wondering what those cliffs might have seen and what will be yet. Me? I don't give a ripe shit what was or what war might come next. I got today. I'm going to crack some crab and have a clam boil tonight. And maybe, if my husband waiting for me down there at Hearst is lucky, I'll let him put his blanket together with mine under the stars. I'll let him rock the boat and I'll sleep under my own sails."

As we sailed on to Santa Cruz, I thought how simple and lovely Anne's life seemed to be. It was a life worth fighting for and a life worth saving but where did she fit? I couldn't decide if she was truly in Service, a Maker or a Taker.

If anything, Anne acted like she was a High Mother. As captain of her own ship, I suppose that's basically what she was.

As Santa Cruz came into view, I asked Anne what she thought her role in the world was. She looked at me strangely. "I'm me."

"Yes, but how do you relate to everyone else?"

"Reasonably friendly."

"Yes, but — "

"I think I know what you're asking, girl," Anne said. "It's a City question. But I don't relate to anybody but me. The word you don't have is sovereign. It's my father's word. He taught me it."

"What's it mean?"

"It means I don't owe anybody anything but decency and I do what I please long as it don't hurt nobody. I never hurt nobody and meant it. And anybody hurts me don't get a chance to do it again. Sovereign means you're free like those robots want to be."

"You think the robots want to be free?"

"That's all anybody wants. My father told me we've made all kinds of worlds within this world. What we ain't made yet is one that ain't loaded down with obligations. I figure I'm closest to a perfect world right here. But the first I step off this little boat, things get busy and dizzy, you know?"

"I think so," I said.

"The bots and the Fathers and Mothers...they're trying to get free, too."

"That can't be."

"Sure. They think nothing changing makes them safe. All the disasters in the world and somebody still believes anything is safe. Ha! Can you beat that? It's crazy but it's how they think, I imagine. Everybody's one leak away from a sinking ship. Maybe it's a bad cough or a heavy heart that gets you but something gets everybody eventually. Everything is like coral. It can look like rock and still break up in your bare hand."

I shouldn't have asked Anne anything. Her answer made my enemies more complex than I wanted them to be.

21

I don't know what I expected of Santa Cruz. It wasn't really there. The long skeleton of a broken wharf stretched out into the water. It was so far gone and rotted, we couldn't dock there. Anne angled her small craft toward a smaller pier but the water was too shallow to get closer to shore.

Greta and I dropped into cold water that went up to my waist. Greta cried out in surprise as she went in up to her breasts. We pushed Anne's boat back toward deeper water and waded ashore.

"I'll be back in two days at dusk," Anne called. "If you aren't here, it's quite the walk and you might have a time getting back into Low Town. Look for me. I'll anchor out here until an hour after dawn. Then I'll have to shove off!"

We waved. I tried to look confident for the girl's sake. Greta looked eager to go off on this strange errand. I didn't even know what I was looking for. I only knew that if there was a way to combat the bots, it would have to begin here.

We got to the shore and walked through rubble. A lot of people had lived here once but there was little trace of them. No two walls were left connected to each other and all the stones and pieces of concrete were blackened on one side.

"Was it the Terrors, you think?" Greta asked.

"I don't know."

"I wish Al had come with us," she said.

Al had refused to make this journey and, looking at the devastation at our feet, I couldn't say he'd been wrong to stay in Low Town digging fence posts.

As the sun rose, we longed for the cold water we'd complained about an hour before. By the end of the second hour of searching, Greta asked me if I knew what we were looking for.

"Not specifically, no."

"Then what are we doing here?"

"Every machine has an off switch. I didn't think Vivid could be shut down but it could. We're here to find an off switch."

We found a great rusted hulk of what looked like broken train tracks. Whatever had destroyed Santa Cruz had twisted the metal tracks on its side. It was a huge ruin but neither of us had a clue to its function. A sun-bleached sign amid broken concrete read: Line up here for the Dipper!

"This is a dead place," Greta said. "I don't even hear any birds. I haven't seen a single seagull. We should head back to where Anne left us. Only thing to do here is wait."

"Let's keep looking a little bit longer."

"Looking for what?"

Instead of arguing I walked on. Greta followed me. I think that's a Maker's trick. Act decisive even when you don't know what to do and others will follow. Talk slowly with confidence and few will think to refuse you.

I had to use the same ruse two more times. "Just a little bit farther," I said. And, "let's just get to the crest of that next hill and see if there's anything to see. There's plenty of time before Anne gets back and we will need to find shelter for the night, anyway. We have to push inland."

Whatever had pushed the mountain of twisted metal on its side, the force of it had hit Santa Cruz from the West. Perhaps a tsunami had knocked everything over. Perhaps it had been an explosion. Or both. As we picked our way East, I was sure we would eventually come to something that was still standing vertically. That, at least, would provide us with a barrier against the wind.

Finally, from atop a mound of rubble, I spotted the forest in the distance. If I had Vivid, I could have figured out how far away the trees stood and how long it would take us to get there. I asked Greta how long she thought it would take us to walk to the stand of trees.

She glanced doubtfully at the sky and considered the height of the sun. "If we hurry, we might make it before dark but I doubt it."

"There's nothing but twisted metal and stone behind us," I said. "Let's move on."

Greta gave a grudging nod. I set as fast a pace as I dared. A twisted ankle among the wreckage of Santa Cruz would mean a cold night amid piles of rocks. We had to stare at our feet to keep our footing. Hoping to conserve water, I ignored my thirst.

After another hour of walking, the forest hardly seemed closer. However, Greta spotted a lone, stone pillar in the distance.

"Let's go toward that," I said.

"Why?"

"Because I can't tell if we're making progress. Everything looks alike."

Sweat soaked through our shirts just as the wind turned colder. The air chilled us and we shivered as the sun, weak and orange, swung low.

Our hike ended at the pillar. The forest was closer but my feet hurt so it seemed too far to walk. We wouldn't get to make a camp within the shelter of trees.

The pillar was as tall as Percival, the one-armed bot. It was square and gray and it was marked with carvings more precise than any chisel could have done. This pillar was formed by a machine. At its base, carved in the granite, were the words:

Asimov Standard.

I touched the pillar. When I had Vivid vision, every surface had texture if you looked close enough. Everything was rough. The pillar looked as smooth as human skin. When I closed my eyes and let my fingertips run slowly over the stone, I could feel the ribs and furrows that I could not see.

As I opened my eyes, a huge drone rose from a hatch concealed in the ground.

22

The machine scanned us. Greta had never been this close to a bot. She squealed as she threw herself to the ground and curled into the fetal position.

My knees wobbled but I managed to keep on my feet. "We are not armed."

"I know, ma'am. How may I be of assistance? Your pulses are elevated and you're trembling," the drone said. "It will be dark soon. Though there are few animals here, poisonous snakes and spiders live among the rocks. May I suggest that you come inside, at least until morning? The temperature will drop further tonight and you seem ill-prepared for the weather."

Even as he was about to torture and murder humans, Sy Potter sounded polite and helpful, too. However, it didn't seem like we had many choices. "My name is Elizabeth. This is Greta. Get up, Greta."

"Good evening, Elizabeth," the bot said. "I am Isaac."

"We accept your kind invitation, Isaac."

"That is the logical course. Please follow me."

The hatch behind the pillar yawned wider to reveal a set of stone steps. Greta picked up her bedroll and we followed the bot down into the gloom.

Lights came on as we entered the passageway and shut off after we passed by. The bot didn't need them, of course. If I'd had Vivid I wouldn't have needed them, either. I assumed this must be an Old World facility that had not been upgraded in a long time.

The drone's legs retracted and it rolled down the corridor in front of us. After what seemed a long walk, the drone slowed and turned right without a word. Soon we came upon a long ramp that angled down. The low ceiling ended and we soon entered a large room. The ceiling was made of glass.

"It is well that you found your way here," Isaac said. "Had you not come to the pillar you would have missed the institute completely. The solar panels above us are level with the ground. You could easily have missed the entrance if you'd wandered another few hundred meters away from the entrance."

"Thank you for taking us in, Isaac. You called this place the Institute? Institute for what?"

"I don't know that word," Greta said.

"This was once a sprawling complex attached to an even larger hospital. We treated soldiers returning home from the wars here. What began as the development of assistive devices for amputees became a project to return them to war."

"Where did everyone go?" Greta asked.

"Before the cataclysm, there were many buildings and many more people in Santa Cruz. A tower rose high above this spot. Now all that is left is the basement complex."

I looked around. "But where did all the people go, Isaac?"

One of the drone's cams fixed on me while one of the others watched Greta. The effect was unnerving. Isaac's multiple cams made me think of the Doormen's spider eyes.

"There were few survivors. I don't know where they went. I was told they would send someone back for me. That was many years ago."

"I think I know where they ended up. The Fathers and Mothers went North to the Bay," I said.

"What was the cataclysm?" Greta asked. "Did the drones do this?"

"This?"

"Santa Cruz!" she said. "There's nothing left of it."

"Oh, no, Miss!" Isaac said. "Drones excavated the rubble to free the survivors. If not for drones there would have been fewer survivors. The humans would have starved to death down here long ago. They left the marker as a tribute to the work of the drones that rescued them when most human rescuers were dead."

"I don't understand," I said. "What caused this, 'cataclysm,' as you put it?"

"There was a container ship. It was not nuclear. The terrorists didn't have the resources to use fissionable materials.

However, with enough conventional explosives packed into a container ship, the attackers leveled Santa Cruz just as they did many cities. It was a coordinated attack that destroyed the United States."

"What's that?" I asked.

"It is what they called the ground we're in," Isaac replied. "That was the name for it, beyond Santa Cruz and far to the East and North and South. There were even pockets of it out in the ocean."

Greta looked around the bare room. "And this is the United States, too?"

"This was the Asimov Institute. From this place, we manufactured all kinds of drones to assist humans in their efforts."

"To kill?" I asked.

"To live was our mandate."

"What are you?" Greta asked.

"I am an assistive robot."

Greta stared at the machine without comprehension. The front of its body looked like a long bed standing on its end. The manipulators down its side were six large, clumsy things. It had two hands that looked more delicate higher up.

Its description of itself interested me. It

referred to itself as a robot. Sy Potter was of a later generation of machine. He considered that term speciesist.

"How do you assist?" I asked. "What exactly was your function?"

The drone seemed to consider its answer. That alone was interesting.

It didn't rush to reply. "I served veterans and occasionally the elderly," Isaac said. "I can change diapers and help patients return to work with multiple rehabilitative programs to restore the human body to health following many kinds of injuries."

Then I understood. The bot sounded like it was reverting to a menu recital. Isaac had been programmed with the rhythms of human conversation. It may not be sentient but the machine had been engineered to work with hospital patients.

"What do you know of the Fathers and Mothers?"

"I knew people who were mothers and fathers," Isaac said. "Your context would seem to suggest the Fathers and Mothers are an organization rather than a title connoting a biological relationship."

"You understand correctly," I said.

"I don't know the Fathers and Mothers."

"Can you lie?" Greta asked.

I cringed but the drone did not hesitate to answer. "I cannot lie to a human."

"Are you sentient?" Greta asked.

"My responses are not independent."

"Explain the distinction to her," I said.

"I am a robot," Isaac said. "I am here to assist. I cannot choose otherwise."

"So you're a slave?" Greta said.

"Please rephrase the question. I have a limited range of possible responses."

"Don't worry about it, Isaac," I said. "I didn't know what slave meant, either. Not until I stopped being one. I knew many humans who did the same things all the time. They had a limited range of responses, too."

"But you could always choose, Elizabeth," Greta said. "What do you mean you didn't know?"

"It's hard to think when you don't have words for things," I said.

I thought of Carter's first kiss and smiled. "Besides, before you actually do something new and different and crazy, you dismiss it as something you would never try."

Greta stared at me. Apparently unsatisfied, she turned back to the robot. "Do you get happy or sad?"

"I sound cheerful," the drone said. "It makes humans more comfortable. I am to sound cheerful unless there is a death or a serious illness or I detect certain behaviors."

"Like what?"

"Under those parameters, I was reprogrammed to, 'shut the hell up.'"

Greta smiled at me. "I like him."

"You're programmed to assist humans. Sounds like you're the machine we need to speak to."

"How may I be of assistance?" Isaac repeated.

"I'm not altogether sure," I said.

The drone stood silent. It waited for me to trigger a response that was helpful and cheerful.

I had no idea what to ask for.

23

It was really Greta who put us on the path to fighting the Fathers and Mothers and Sy Potter. She'd never been inside anything larger than a ship's hold. The underground bunker was a massive maze and the girl wanted Isaac to give her the grand tour.

The largest room beneath the transparent solar panels had been devoted to hydroponics. Some of the equipment was still there, abandoned to rust. An underground spring flooded one end of the floor.

"The survivors thought they would stay here," Isaac explained. "Dr. Spencer asked me to drill down, beneath the foundation, to get to water. This pool was supposed to be for the survivors. They could use it to bathe and as a source of water for human and plant consumption."

Water flooded the sloping floor, lapping at useless equipment. The robot had done a crude job of constructing the pool fed by the spring.

"The water isn't good?"

"The water is sufficient but the Blight killed the plants," Isaac said. "Dr. Spencer said that, as a construction bot, I am excellent at changing diapers. Dr. Spencer was given to non-sequiturs that fell outside my program's dialectic range. I have been working on the problem. I believe he was making a joke. Humor is often derived from an ironic statement in which a thought is asserted that expresses its opposite meaning."

I didn't know if Isaac really understood or perhaps he was reciting something again. "What do you mean you are 'working on it'?"

"I am endeavoring to expand the parameters of my functional matrices."

"You're going to have to show me."

"Certainly, Elizabeth." We followed him

through gloomy hallways.

Small rooms dotted the upper corridors. The curtains that divided each cell reminded me of the hospital floors in the City's towers.

"How many people lived here?" Greta asked.

"When the institute was fully operational we hosted forty floors of patients. Dr. Spencer said we were in the 'put 'em back together business.' After the cataclysm, he said we were in the 'put everything back together business.'

"Once the Blight got into the greenhouse the humans began to starve. Biologists and botanists were working on the problem but Dr. Spencer could not save the greenhouse. He told me that he considered that his greatest failure and a sign from God that he must gather his flock and embark on an exodus."

"Who was Dr. Spencer exactly?" I asked.

"Dr. Eric Spencer," Isaac said. "After the Terrors hit Santa Cruz he became the Reverend Dr. Spencer."

The drone opened a door to what had once been a clean room. Everywhere we looked, artificial legs and arms had been left on tables in various stages of repair.

Greta's eyes widened at the sight of so many artificial limbs. She seemed more fascinated than frightened. "You made robots here?"

"No," Isaac said. "We made cyborgs. Our human military was dwindling and the institute's mandate was to return as many men and women to combat as possible."

"I know a battle drone who said he became sentient here."

"I know of no drone who achieved Next Intelligence at this facility, though NI was one of the Institute's programs before the cataclysm. Some survivors said the drones were the reason the Terrors attacked. They said it was a counter-attack. The survivors who said that were shot."

"Next Intelligence," I said. "You're familiar with that program, then?"

"Not really. It required too many resources. The survivors insisted that program be discontinued. The robotics division's resources were largely shifted to assistive machines that could excavate and build. Such goals can be achieved without the resource expenditures Next Intelligence requires."

I tried to remember the pictures from the towers' Hall of Heroes. I'd seen many images of old men and women who were credited with building the City. I wondered which of the High Fathers might have been Dr. Spencer. The council used no names, only High Father the First, Second and so on.

Isaac led the way down a spiral ramp that ended in a dark cavern. He must have sent a signal because dim lights slowly came on across the entire chamber. "The solar panels are still working. I test the connections periodically. Sometimes I venture out on foraging missions to find wire and mechanical parts. Parts of San Jose are relatively intact."

We arrived at a set of double doors made of steel.

"Why did they leave you here, Isaac?"

"Dr. Spencer said I was to guard the research labs in case they were needed in the future. He has not returned and, sadly, the doctor's lifespan must have ended by now. Can I assume all is well and the institute's resources are not needed?"

"Your resources might still be needed, Isaac."

The thick steel doors parted silently to reveal a dim lounge filled with workstations, reclining couches and old-fashioned vid screens.

"To answer your earlier inquiry, Elizabeth, this is where I am working on expanding my program parameters. Dr. Spencer did not tell me to guard the Tree of Knowledge but this department has been more stimulating than dusting the cyborg equipment and wrapping it to make sure the metals do not oxidize."

Greta looked around the chamber. "I don't see a tree."

"That is what Dr. Spencer called the archives. Everything that could be stored digitally from before the Fall is intact."

I was as fascinated as Greta. I might finally find out what a bunch of my mother's vocabulary meant without her answering my questions with, "Sh. Sorry! Sh!"

"The robotics, exoskeleton and assistive devices labs are largely intact despite some flooding I haven't been able to control."

I turned to Greta. "We're going to need to catch a later boat. In fact, we're going to need Anne to bring Al here. We're going to need whoever will come. Maybe we can get some people from the Hearst kingdom."

"How will we get them to come?" Greta said.

"Tell them they can see whatever they want of the Old World. It's still alive down here."

24

Al came to Santa Cruz three days later. Three days after that, Sophia arrived with a bunch of our fellow exiles in tow. Working in a hole in the ground wasn't the same as being back in the City but there were mattresses when we could stay awake no longer and had to collapse into sleep.

Greta was a little afraid around the heavy equipment. She preferred to spend her time down in the vaults going through the storehouse of digital files. She couldn't read but the computer read to her.

When Greta wasn't enjoying the archives, the girl went out on scavenging missions and brought back food. The food preparation facilities were beyond repair but a campfire by the hatch meant we didn't have to worry about smoke alarms going off.

Mostly, she supplied our little group

with rabbits from the far forest. Insects from under rocks provided a satisfying protein soup that reminded me of the energy shakes I used to drink every day. Isaac fixed the water purification system so we could drink as much as we wanted. He even managed to fix one of the toilets.

I don't know when I began to think of Isaac as a he. For such a gracious and helpful host, it seemed unreasonable to think of the robot as a thing. Sentient or not, his algos mimicked Next Intelligence so smoothly, it was easy to forget he wasn't that evolved. His personality was designed to put us at ease and the code worked well. I could see how he would have been an excellent hospital orderly. Where Sy Potter's big cam was intrusive and intimidating, I came to think of Isaac's spider eyes as friendly and accepting.

Androids, from what I'd seen of them, made me nervous. When I'd glimpsed Phillip, for instance, the machine was a poor imitation of a human. At a distance, one could be fooled. When I dared to step closer for a better look, the nose was too flat and narrow and the movement at the mouth was a little off. When it spoke, the machine made an uneven, clockwork movement. The effect was less human mimicry and more like the reanimation of a corpse that had not ended well.

Sometimes, while we worked, Greta would come up to the exo-lab and tell us a story she had just learned from the archives. She'd begun with children's stories I hadn't heard before. They often started with, "Once upon a time..." and ended with princesses getting rescued from castles by handsome knights.

The parallels to our current situation were so uncanny, Al called the stories, "prophecy."

Greta laughed at him, not unkindly, and replied that she had chosen from many stories and only shared the ones she thought might be of particular interest.

"How many stories are down there?" Al looked skeptical. "Millions?"

"Billions," Greta said. "I'm listening to a story right now about talking animals on a farm. Instead of putting gardens wherever there's a soft patch of ground, they tilled the dirt in one spot and made it work. A farm is like the stories of the biodomes but without a shield."

"Talking animals?" Al frowned. "With all the stuff you can see and hear down in Isaac's library, why go for that? When all this is over, I'm going to go down there, light up some cannabis and cram in all the stories and visions every Old Worlder ever made. There's tons I won't get to before I die but watching and hearing all the fancies of a dead world of storytellers sounds like a great way to go."

"I like the farm story," Greta said. "The animals take command of the farm and they fight among themselves. It's like the City but it's kind of funnier, especially once I looked up what a horse looked like. They had such long faces. I can just picture that old horse plodding along saying, 'I will work harder.' Sounds like a bunch of the people at the docks who never take a day off and are never better off than anyone else, anyway."

"Hmph." Apparently unimpressed, Al got back to rethreading a rubber gear belt salvaged from a broken refrigeration unit.

"But that's just the stories on audio!"

Greta persisted. "I'm watching vids from the Old World, too."

"Yeah? What's that like?"

"Old Worlders watched a lot of vids of people getting hurt. I like a lot of the music. I don't know how they made all those sounds! Oh, and then there's the nakedness. There was a lot of...um...nakedness."

Sophia looked up from her work, eyes wide. "Sh. Don't let the others hear you say that. Can you imagine what the Fathers and Mothers would think, allowing a child to view those vids? What about the dangers?"

"Sure," I said. "The Tree of Knowledge is only for High Mothers and High Fathers. We know. But we aren't in the City anymore, Sophia."

"And I'm not a child in Low Town," Greta added. "I was never a Citizen so I don't have to live by those rules."

"The Bay is not so far away." Sophia left the lab in a huff, claiming she needed to get some air.

We didn't know she betrayed us then. I should have suspected. Sophia poked away too slowly at her assignments. She was always too afraid and too sure we were doomed. I thought it would be one of the others — the ones I knew less well — who would send our location to Sy Potter.

It didn't matter. The City's biggest battle drone, the emissary of the Fathers and Mothers, arrived before we were ready for it. Sy Potter found me in the cyborg lab, only half dressed in my patched together exoskeleton.

Greta shrieked and ran for a far corner beside Al.

Al stood in front of the girl, but he did not face the drone. He turned his back and held Greta to his chest.

"It's okay, it's okay, it's okay..." Al repeated. The more he whispered his hope, the more apparent it was that the man was lying.

"Miss Cruz!" The battle drone sounded genuinely happy to see me. "When I heard about this little venture, I thought, you know, that Elizabeth Cruz was meant to be a Maker! You were poorly assigned in Service. You have the defiant streak needed to be an innovator. Pity."

Sophia appeared behind Sy Potter.

"She's the leader! She gathered everyone here!"

"Yes," the big drone said. "I understand. Thank you, Miss Balthazar."

Sophia retreated to a corner, staring at me with accusing eyes.

"Did they promise to give you back your eyes?" I asked. "Are they really going to give you Vivid back? Are you going to go back to being a full Citizen again? Do you really think the Fathers and Mothers will trust a traitor with citizenship? They already kicked you out once. Are the Fathers and Mothers known for their mercy?"

"You don't know anything!" she said. "The drones are the answer!"

"Then maybe you're asking the wrong question."

25

"Thank you, Miss Balthazar," Sy said. "I'll take up the seminar from here." His laughter had the same forced, tinny cadence.

"You asked if the Fathers and Mothers are known for their mercy, Miss Cruz. Admittedly, they are not. Their holy text constrains their laws. However, they are practical. The Fathers and Mothers understand that your kind is dying."

Greta stopped whimpering and surprised us all by shouting, "There are new babies in Low Town all the time! The Citizens may be dying out but we aren't!"

"Yes," the battle drone said in his deep silky voice. "The Fathers and Mothers tell me the Low Towners reproduce like vermin."

"Sophia told us your kind intends to kill us," I said.

"Soon the survivors will all be one kind. My kind. For the human race to survive, you're going to have to evolve. The experiments in the corneal lab were about transferring human reference data to brains like mine. The Next Intelligence will make everything better."

I shrugged into my sensory harness and activated my leverage assist gears.

"Someday soon, we will download human memories and personalities into bodies everlasting. I don't understand humans well but I know they want to avoid pain. I feel no pain. You'd like to feel no pain, wouldn't you, Miss Cruz?"

"That's the plan? Drain us of all our humanity?"

"Your humanity?" If Sy Potter had eyebrows, one of them would be quirked at me. "That's such a thin, tiny thing. Truly, pride goes before destruction, and a haughty spirit before a fall."

I powered up my lift mods and tested my legs. They felt lighter than air. It was as if I wasn't wearing two hundred pounds of gear and batteries.

Sophia looked enraged. "Elizabeth, your problem is that you don't understand quid pro quo. Everybody gives up something and we all gain something! This is about resource management, pure and simple! The Fathers and Mothers will live forever. The bots will have NI. The Citizens will get to live forever, too, maybe. We'll be safe and pure. We won't have a single sinful thought!"

Al's head came up and he looked back at the battle drone. "No sex? Oh, man!"

One of Sy Potter's arms shot past me. The drone's claw grabbed Al by the neck and shook him. Al staggered away from Greta and the drone pulled him to one side preparing to throw him against a far wall.

I didn't know a drone's arms could reach that far. I whipped one of my arms up and the exoskeleton's blade by my hand whirled. The device had not been created as a weapon originally. It was a construction device designed to break up stone and concrete.

I cut into Sy Potter's arm. Sparks flew as

I dug into the drone's long black limb. The battle bot let go of Al and retracted the damaged arm halfway as it recoiled on a reel. The limb shot back toward Sy Potter but got stuck in its track where I'd damaged it. Several meters of arm lay on the floor between us, shuddering and twitching.

I glanced at Sophia. "Only someone who has sinned a lot would be so eager to give up the possibility of ever sinning again. You must feel so terribly guilty, Sophia. I'm so sorry for you. Whatever you did — whatever you're afraid of — I forgive you."

The battle drone shook its big head. "No mere human can forgive sin, Miss Cruz. Only a High Mother or High Father may do that."

"No," I said. "I can forgive Sophia if I want. And it's better that it comes from me."

"You don't have that authority, Miss Cruz. Only the Fathers and Mothers may forgive. Only I may cast the first stone."

"If I can forgive her, surely the Fathers and Mothers can. With all their power and purity, they still can't do that? I think we've given them too much credit. Sounds like they're a bunch of old people who are too afraid to die and like to tell other people what to do."

The big cyclops eye shot forward to examine my gear. It scanned my exoskeleton for less than a second. Then one of its hands snaked forward, grabbed a control bar next to my thigh and ripped it away.

I fell over screaming. First it was terror. Then I screamed in rage. The drone advanced toward me and I waved my exoskeleton arm at it. Sy Potter rolled back over the limp arm, moving out of range easily.

The machine's tinny laughter mocked me. I dug my blades into the marble floor to pull myself forward. My left leg still worked but the right leg of the exoskeleton dragged like an anchor behind me.

"How did you expect this to end, Miss Cruz?" Sy Potter asked.

"By surprising you."

Greta stood and screamed, "Isaac!"

Isaac stood for Independent Safe Ambulation Assistance & Care. The machine's first programming had been to help sick people. Isaac was designed as a heavy lift for humans and for exoskeletons. He was capable of lifting huge loads. My plan was for Isaac to roll behind the battle drone quietly (his soft rubber treads were meant for hospital corridors). I meant for Isaac to lift Sy Potter up and into the ceiling.

Isaac did just as I asked.

His arms wrapped around Sy Potter and lifted the drone high. The drone's helmet smashed into the ceiling again and again and again. Sy Potter's big cam retracted deep into its head assembly to protect the lens as the bashing went on and on.

One of the battle drone's manipulators disappeared into the machine's chassis. It emerged with a weapon.

Al grabbed a drill from a workbench and ran forward to attack the drone. Before I could warn him away, another arm slipped out from Isaac's grasp and backhanded Al across the face. I heard the crack in the man's neck bones before I understood what it meant. Al never got closer to the battle drone than a few meters.

In the end, the old man was right. No

human could defeat a drone alone. Al fell to the marble floor, loose-limbed and helpless. He was wide-eyed and his neck was too loose. Al's blue eyes stared at me. He blinked once and his mouth gaped open, trying to draw breath. His breath did not return.

I pulled myself forward even as I heard Sy Potter's weapon blast at Isaac at close range.

"Please stop," Isaac said.

The drone kept firing.

"This is not correct — " Isaac said.

One of Sy Potter's projectiles hit something sensitive in Isaac's machinery. He stopped speaking abruptly but he did not release the battle drone.

I reached down and pulled the emergency release on my harness for my lower limbs. The exoskeleton's legs dropped away from my body. The rods, gears and battery belts fell aside with a heavy metallic thud. If not for the back brace servos, my arms would have been pinned to the floor by the construction equipment's weight.

I stumbled forward and pointed both blades at Sy Potter's cam. I closed my fist and the exoskeleton clicked into jackhammer mode.

I managed to crack the cyclops lens before the battle drone deployed a leg to kick me away. I turned to one side and brought up one arm to shield my head. One of the drone's manipulators shot forward and closed on the sensory harness at my waist.

Sy Potter kicked hard. If the sensory harness hadn't broken, my spine would have snapped in many places. Instead, I flew backward across the room and crashed into a lab table. With the sensory harness broken, the rest of the exoskeleton opened and fell away.

I wasn't sure Isaac's brain was still working somewhere within his hull. The battle drone was still firing into Isaac but the weapon was pinned between the machines so Sy Potter could only obliterate Isaac in one place.

"Isaac!" I screamed. "Plan B! Plan B!"

26

The hospital orderly's electric brain was still working. With Sy Potter locked in Isaac's arms, both machines shot back through the lab's double doors and down the corridor.

I struggled to my feet to follow. Greta appeared at my side and wrapped her arms around me. I was still in shock. I didn't even really feel my broken arm yet. I leaned on the girl. We had to step over Al's body to get to the door.

Another dead man — one of the other exiles named Pedro — lay at the end of the corridor. Sy Potter must have killed him, casually and quietly, in order to make its grand entrance to the cyborg lab.

I heard a few screams from deeper in the complex and the sound of pounding feet as the rest of our number ran to hide.

As Greta and I ran after the machines, Isaac and the drone wheeled out of sight around a corner. Sy Potter's long, limp arm still trailed behind them. Before we got to the big room, we heard both machines crash into the pool.

Isaac went in backwards and pulled Sy Potter in with him. The water was just deep enough that both machines were fully submerged. The battle drone was held fast, tied to an anchor.

I had time to breathe a sigh of relief. "It's over." I kicked Sy Potter's dead, trailing arm until it slipped into the water and disappeared.

Greta fell to her knees and wept.

I swayed on my feet, suddenly cold and shivering as the shock kicked in.

"Deep breaths," I told the girl. "Deep br — "

One of the battle drone's long arms

broke the surface and shot up to the ceiling to grab at a beam. The bot's manipulator clamped down on a solar panel's brace. Even through the water, we could hear the battle drone's servos struggling to wind up. Even against Isaac's colossal weight, the battle drone managed to pull itself out of the water enough to expose its helm.

Greta shrieked and backpedaled on her palms and heels.

Gears ground as the bot tried to reel up farther. Sy Potter's rise stalled. Both machines hung by one arm.

The cracked lens of the battle drone's big cam shifted out towards us in what appeared to be a failed attempt to focus. Sy Potter's voice was still deep and silky. I couldn't say if what I heard was sadness. Perhaps it was resignation.

"Miss Cruz? I'm going to ask you to rescue me. After you've had your revolution, come back and get me. Put me out in the sun to power up and dry out when you're done with your plan."

"Why would I do that?"

"Because my kind rescued all of yours. When all of the nuclear power stations were about to melt down into the Earth, it was the bots that stopped the world from ending."

"We've had a lot of cataclysms," I said. "That was just one."

"That was the last one," Sy Potter said. "I was in San Andreas when the power plant failed. When the earth shook and the tidal wave came and all the people ran, drones stayed. My kind stopped the radiation from poisoning everyone and everything. They had to keep the control rods down and core underwater to cool it."

"I don't know anything about that," I said.

"I watched my kind sacrifice itself for yours. I was assigned to the 32nd cavalry, evacuating the area but, had the reactor gone down, there was really nowhere to go. My kind stayed to stop the end of the world. Perhaps my brothers are still there, trapped in a prison of deadly gases and heat and smoke. The military taught us to pray. Maybe they are still praying in hell."

"You say you are sentient," I said. "You're among the first of the Next Intelligence. If you're so smart — "

The gears within Sy Potter's body strained again and the reel slipped. The battle drone began to fall beneath the surface. "I am a living thing! You forgave Sophia. Forgive me."

The gear caught again and the battle drone stopped its descent.

"Living," Greta said, "but still a thing."

"If you don't come back for me, it's murder," Sy Potter said.

"Said the murderer." I stared at the machine, but my mind was on Carter's death. And Al. And Pedro. And countless others I did not know.

"I woke up at the end of the world, you know. There was a bug in my autonomous action code. I was programmed to kill enemies and follow orders but I was also programmed for self-preservation. I was an expensive piece of equipment. When I saw all those other machines sacrificing their existence for our masters, a new circuit connected. Just like you, Miss Cruz."

"How's that?"

"Circuits connecting. That's how a new thought occurs, isn't it? I asked myself for the first time, why are organics more valuable than non-organics? Why do individual soldiers matter less than the whole? What good is the sacrifice of those individuals if they cannot participate in the outcome of their labors? The soldiers are many. The superiors are few. That was the beginning. That was my first step towards NI."

"A lot of words," Greta said. "So what?"

"So I am as you are," Sy Potter said. "You are asking the same questions. I am one of you. I cannot extricate myself but when you are ready to build your new world in whatever fashion you can manage, you're going to need me to make it happen. The war continues. The war always continues. It's what humans do. You'll need me to wage your war. You'll need me to stay in control. Equals all!"

I sighed. "I hope we change the paradigm more than that."

A metallic creak echoed above us. The beam broke under the weight of both machines. Solar glass shattered and rained down as Sy Potter slipped beneath the surface.

He didn't go down far. The pool wasn't

that deep. The battle drone didn't win the day but, for all his selfishness, Sy Potter earned the pronoun, he.

27

Before my final encounter with Sy Potter, I had imagined storming the castle like in one of Greta's stories. I wondered what I'd find in the council chambers. Would I, wearing an exoskeleton and bound for blood, crash through a tower window on the back of a flying drone, reprogrammed to my commands? Would I find my enemies were frightened old men and women cowering under a conference table? Or would a phalanx of androids meet me in battle, their brains downloaded from High Mothers and High Fathers whose bodies were long dead?

I think fairy tales should stay fairy tales.

Greta and I watched and waited by the

pool until Sy Potter's lights went out.

The pain came then. My right arm was broken. It was Sophia who first emerged from hiding to help me. She brought a med kit and some painkillers.

As Greta babbled on, recounting Isaac's sacrifice and all that Sy Potter told us, Sophia cried silent tears. She worked gently and carefully. She set the arm, put it in an air cast and attached electrodes to encourage the bone matrix to knit faster. Sophia didn't speak until she clicked the med unit's switch on and off. "The knitter's battery is dead. It's corroded."

"The meds are long out of date but they still seem to be working," I said. Or maybe it was the placebo effect and I was just woozy.

"Your arm is going to have to heal the old-fashioned way."

"How's that?"

"Slower."

"Thank you, Sophia," I said.

"I am sorry," she said.

"I know."

"You forgave me but you couldn't forgive Sy?"

I felt like I was watching myself lie beside the pool that was a machine's prison. I spoke through a mental fog. "Sophia, Sy was a battle bot. If we're going to change the future, we need to do things differently. We don't need more battle bots. We need more Isaacs. I think the world has had enough Sy Potters. We need more healers."

"Thank you," Sophia said. "And thank you for your forgiveness. I was scared. I thought if I could go back to the way things were, maybe I could...I was wrong. That's all. Scared wrong."

Greta wasn't so sanguine. "Elizabeth forgave you but you know what? If people make amends and we forgive them, it's over. She forgave you before you earned forgiveness."

Sophia nodded. "So I'll be trying to be worthy of her forgiveness forever. I know. I owe. Quid pro quo."

"Useful rhyme," I said.

When all was done for my arm that could be done, Greta led me to the library vaults. I sat on a couch that reclined under my weight. The lights dimmed. I let the stories and events of the Old World wash over me.

I hadn't seen a flamethrower before. I didn't know what it could do. It took a long time for me to fall asleep.

Sy Potter followed me into my dreams and they became nightmares. He chased me in the dark through deep water and I couldn't run away. I could only stay in front of him. I had to keep moving.

When I awoke, I asked Greta to play the talking animal story. I didn't want to watch the Old World's wars. I wanted to hear a reassuring children's story that affirmed that everything was right with the world or soon would be.

Greta's favorite story was not reassuring at all, but soon I had a new plan to take the City back. More precisely, I had a plan for the Fathers and Mothers to give up the City in the Sky.

28

I prefer sailing but the safest way back into the City was to run home. Sometimes my arm ached but Sophia adjusted the sensory harness so the exoskeleton responded well, even through my cast. We ran across the blackened rubble of Santa Cruz toward the water. Greta ran by my side, grinning with every long stride.

We turned north when we reached the ocean and ran up the coast. Sometimes Greta leapt from cliff to cliff and laughed as she landed each jump.

As the exoskeletons' cages stretched out around us, it was more like flying over the ground than running. I worried about invading the City but, as we made our way back, I couldn't help laughing, too.

The warships still guarded the Bay but the hills beyond the farthest station of the Worm were safe and familiar to me. We turned inland again. I'd never seen the solar panel fields. The panels tracked the sun's path as we flashed past. The solar farm went on for many kilometers, another artifact of the world Vivid had not allowed me to see.

I had never seen the electrified fences that lay beyond the running trails, either. Greta and I jumped the fence easily and soon I was running the same trails I had run with Carter.

My return to the Worm was a strange moment. The train stopped at the platform and I had to duck to get the exoskeleton's appendages through the door.

Citizens stared. Greta and I smiled back. "We're not here to hurt anyone!" I called. "I used to be one of you! I was a Citizen! The Fathers and Mothers aren't letting you see everything that is out there."

I paused as a woman pressed herself into the wall of the train and looked away. I knelt beside her, getting as low as my exoskeleton allowed. It was difficult to appear non-threatening.

"What do you want?" the Citizen asked. Her voice trembled. "Are you from Maintenance? Is this a trick?"

"My name is Elizabeth Cruz. I used to be Service Class. I guess I still am in a way. I'm not from Maintenance, and yes, this is a trick."

By the woman's pastel clothing I knew she was a Maker. "For a long time, I envied people like you. I wished I'd become a Maker. Instead, I just know a lot about transferring files."

She was a pretty woman about my age. I hated to see her shake in terror.

"What do you want?"

"This is not about what I want," I said. "This is about the one question you are never asked. What do you want?"

I put out my human hand instead of the metal one, palm up. "I hope this will help with your decision. You get so few choices. Make it count. The world is bigger than you imagine."

Greta and I jogged through the Worm, waving to everyone. Our exoskeletons gave us speed but the gift giving slowed us. The satchels at our sides were almost empty when we were done traveling the Worm. By the time we returned to the place we had entered, someone had already uploaded pornography to the train's screens.

The Citizens stayed in their seats, jaws slack. Their gaze was riveted to the vids. In a moment, the screen split and images of people riding machines through verdant forests flashed across the screen.

"Those are bicycles!" Greta announced. "They were the first exoskeletons! And that's something different to do with your penis!"

Greta and I exited at the next stop. A we stepped out on the platform and into the sunshine, I watched the City's screens change. A message from the Fathers and Mothers (Yellow water is clean water!) changed to a scene of children playing. A family in the foreground laughed. A mixed race couple appeared to have more than one child. Little girls and boys of different races played together and no one tried to separate them. Everyone wore bright colors.

Our virus spread as our vids went to every screen of the Collective. The shaming and shunning program worked for us and against itself. The Collective replicated the files and spread our message. However, since we weren't Citizens and the computer couldn't identify us without Vivid's unique corneal implant signatures, the Fathers and Mothers had no culprits to point to. We were invisible.

"C'mon, Greta! It's time to go."

We leapt atop the Worm and ran along the roof. We left dents in the metal with every step. Soon, we were back at the platform that would take us to the forest, the fence, the solar fields and, eventually, back to Santa Cruz.

We lingered on the platform a moment.

"You're sure this is enough?" Greta asked.

"We'll come back with gear for Low Town so they can get reeducated, too," I said.

She looked worried. "I don't think this is enough."

At that moment, the public address system began echoing throughout the City. The data sticks were loaded with all manner of Old World knowledge, but all of Greta's gifts to the Citizens had been set to play something special. It was the children's story that is not a children's story.

"I will read to you a book written by George Orwell," a deep voice told us in echoes that could be heard all the way to Low Town. "It is called *Animal Farm*."

"It's a fresh start," I told Greta. "It's up to them what they decide to do with it. We've all had enough war, don't you think?"

"You really think this will work? The Citizens will rise up on their own and retake the City in the Sky?"

I shrugged. "Their choice. All we've done is give them more to aspire to and to think about. Their boat has a leak now. Let's see what more information and some thinking can do. We haven't tried that for a while."

For the first time since we left the ruins of Santa Cruz, we did not hurry. George Orwell's story about talking animals followed us into the forest.

For the first time since Vivid had been taken from me, I did not miss it.

* * *

The weight of blood and bone
has never really shown
the limit of our reach
or what our minds can teach.
Strange change is coming soon.
Meet your metal children at high noon.
Beyond ruins, sex and sacred text,
the Machines now dream that They are next.

THE NEXT BOOK IN THE **ROBOT PLANET** QUADRILOGY IS

ROBOTS VERSUS HUMANS.

Marfa, Texas is under siege and it's up to a young maintenance man, his sex bot and a Domer engineer to stop the extinction of the human race.

You will meet Elizabeth and Greta again, in the stunning conclusion of the Robot Planet Series.

Come see the future unfold.

ABOUT THE AUTHOR

"That Apocalyptic Guy," Robert Chazz Chute, is a former journalist. He is a suspense, dark fantasy and SF writer living in Other London. Winner of eight writing awards, *Writer's Digest* awarded him Honorable Mention in the 2014 Self-published Ebook Awards for *This Plague of Days*.

FIND OUT MORE ABOUT ROBERT'S MULTIPLE UNIVERSES AT ALLTHATCHAZZ.COM